Meant to Be

Meant to Be

Be

JO KNOWLES

CANDLEWICK PRESS

First edition 2022

Library of Congress Catalog Card Number 2021946598
ISBN 978-1-5362-1032-3

21 22 23 24 25 26 LBM 10 9 8 7 6 5 4 3 2 1

Printed in Melrose Park, IL, USA

This book was typeset in Dante.

Candlewick Press
99 Dover Street
Somerville, Massachusetts 02144

www.candlewick.com

For Phiroz
Friends forever

✪ Chapter One ✪

It was Saaaaa-turrrrrrr-dayyyyyy(!), my favorite day of the week! I had just finished up my business in the bathroom and was heading back to the bedroom I share with my big sister, Rachel, when Dad hollered after me.

"IVY ELEANOR GARTNER, WERE YOU IN HERE? NEXT TIME TURN ON THE FAN!"

I giggled as I danced down the short hall. "Everybody poops!" I sang, hopping on one foot to get the ants out of my pants. That's what my mom calls it when I can't sit still because I'm so excited.

"You are so gross," Rachel said in a sleepy voice when I hopped into our room. "And too loud."

Rachel had just turned fourteen and acted like a real teenager, sleeping late and always complaining about how much I embarrassed her.

"Hmph," I said. "Some people have no sense of humor." I slid aside the purple shower curtain that divides our tiny room in two. Rachel rolled over and pretended to go back to sleep. Booorrrring. She was no fun anymore. Ever since we moved to this apartment a year ago, she'd become a real grump.

Before we moved here, we lived in an old farmhouse my parents had been fixing up. My mom called it a "labor of love," but to me it just seemed like a lot of hard work. She spent all her free time painting walls and sanding floors and doing all kinds of stuff to make the old house look nice. We also had a small garden, so when my parents weren't inside fixing up the house, they were outside weeding and planting and doing chores. They were always busy, busy, busy, with no time to have fun. Then they had some money troubles and the bank took the house away from us, and we had to move here, to Applewood Heights.

Living in the apartment is very different from living at our old place.

First, the apartment is a lot smaller, which means I get to share a room with Rachel. At our house, if I had a bad dream, I had to run to Rachel's room for safety, which was scary because I had to go out to the hallway all by myself in the dark. In our apartment, if I have a bad dream, all I have to do is whisper from my side of the curtain and Rachel will say, "It's OK. It was only a dream." And I feel safe.

Second, and best of all, I have friends right in my own building. At our house, I didn't have any friends in the neighborhood, and in the summer, most of the kids I knew went to camp. It was lonely! Sometimes Rachel and her best friend, Micah, who lived down the street, let me tag along with them, but it wasn't the same as having my own special friend to play with. At Applewood Heights, I have *two* special friends, Alice and Lucas. And anytime I want to see them, all I have to do is hop in the elevator and knock on their doors!

Our cat, George, who'd been sleeping on my bed, stood and stretched. His soft fur was all staticky, and he looked like he'd put his paw in a light socket. He hopped onto Rachel's bed and padded quietly up her side.

"George!" Rachel moaned from under the covers. "Get off!"

I made a face she couldn't see and scooped up George, then slid the curtain back, shutting myself off from Miss Grouch.

It was Rachel who had persuaded my mom to buy

the purple shower curtain to hang between the ends of our beds, which practically touched because the room was so small. The curtain acted like a wall so that Rachel could sort of have her own room. I didn't see why she needed so much privacy.

My mom said we could decorate our sides of the curtain however we'd like. Rachel decorated her side of the curtain with silly emoji faces and pictures of her and Micah. Leaving him was one more reason Rachel was so sour about having to live here. I decorated my side of the curtain by taping up some of my best drawings, including one of George, of course, and our pony, Rainbow. We had to give him away when we moved. He was what I missed most about living at the farmhouse. Even though he was old and lazy, he would let me sit on his back while he ate grass in our yard, and Rachel read to us from a lawn chair. I liked to braid his mane and tell him secrets, as if he was my best friend. Luckily, we found a good home for him at the fancy house across the street. But I still missed him. Whenever I looked at my drawing of him, I felt a twinge of sadness. But I knew he was happy in his new home — just like me!

I changed out of my pjs and into shorts and a T-shirt and left Rachel to go back to sleep. It was my favorite day because I got to watch the cooking show *Bake It to Make It!* with Alice and Lucas.

"Ivy!" my mom called from the living room, where she was drinking coffee with my dad. "What kind of pancakes are you making us?"

"I need to check my options," I said.

"I'm sure whatever you make will be delicious!" my dad called back.

Not to brag, but I knew he was right. Ever since Alice and Lucas got me hooked on *Bake It to Make It!*, I'd learned how to cook all kinds of things. Pancakes were just one of my many specialties.

On the show, three contestants competed each week. They got a small batch of surprise ingredients presented in a pot called "the Pot-Pourri" and had to make something delicious out of them. After the show, Alice, Lucas, and I would gather the same ingredients and try to re-create the winner. Sometimes the ingredients were too expensive or hard to find. When this happened, we let Lucas's dad, Mr. Stevens, choose a surprise replacement.

One time we made something called "Nutsations." The Pot-Pourri ingredients that day were peanuts, butter, and confectionary sugar. We smashed up all the ingredients until they were smooth and then formed the dough into little buttery balls. We shared them with people we knew in the building, and they were a huge hit. Another time we made a treat we called "Beet-Its." The ingredients that week were canned beets, condensed milk, and limes. Those were a lot less popular.

I had one hour to make pancakes before the show started. Plenty of time to create a masterpiece. First, I checked the fruit bowl. There was one too-brown banana and a kiwi that looked fuzzier than it should. *Yuck.* But in the fridge, I found half a jar of raspberry jam. *Perfect.*

I turned on the little radio next to the fridge and did my signature happy dance, which involved a lot of bum wiggling, while I put everything together. My favorite was mixing ingredients with a special flick of the wrist, the way Dustin Kendal, one of the judges of the show, did when he demonstrated how to make something.

"How're the pancakes coming along?" my mom asked as she walked into the kitchen for more coffee.

"I have everything under control," I told her confidently. "You're in for a real treat."

"I wouldn't expect any less," my mom said. She and my dad had only watched the show a few times, but they were both grateful I loved it so much, especially since it meant I'd learned how to make them delicious treats.

I spooned dollops of batter into a pan and waited for the telltale bubbles to form to let me know it was time to flip them over. But before I did, I used a teaspoon to swirl a little jam on top of each one to make a pinwheel design.

"Gor-gee-oh-so!" I said in my best Carly Lin impression. She was the other judge on *Bake It to Make It!* and had a way of adding syllables to words when she wanted to give them extra emphasis.

When the pancakes were ready, I found some maple syrup in the fridge and poured it into a pretty pitcher. Too bad I didn't have real raspberries for a garnish, but they were too expensive.

"Breakfast's ready!" I sang, after I'd plated the pancakes for my parents. That's a fancy word for arranging the food on a plate just so. Dustin and Carly say that how you plate a dish is important because it makes a good first impression.

"Should we get Rachel up?" my mom asked.

"Taste them first," I said. "See if you think they're worth the risk."

"Good idea," my dad said, winking at me.

"Oh, be nice," my mom said. "It's not easy being a teenager."

"Try being nine!" I said. I gave them their plates and passed the maple syrup pitcher.

My dad made a big show of acting like Carly Lin as he cut a small piece of pancake with his knife and fork. He chewed carefully and slowly to make sure he got every piece on his taste buds before swallowing.

My mom took dainty bites the way Dustin Kendal always did. She closed her eyes in concentration while she nibbled and finally swallowed. "Simply divine," she said in Dustin's southern accent.

"A perfect balance of maple and fruit," my dad agreed. "You've got a winner!"

I nodded, unsurprised. Then I made myself a plate and joined them at the table, which was way too big for the space and took up most of the dining area. My mom had insisted on keeping it because my dad had made it from the wood of an old pine tree that had fallen on our property at the farmhouse.

My mom seemed to miss the house more than any of the rest of us, even Rachel. Once I saw her running her hand along the table, as if she was remembering a special meal we'd all shared there, and it gave me a horrible ache in my chest. It seemed like my family was always remembering how special our old place was and wishing we were still back there. No one seemed to think we could fill *this* place with special memories, too.

Whenever they talked about moving again, it made me feel scared and worried, like I felt the last time we moved. I'd put my fingers in my ears and sing, "La, la, la, I can't hear you!" to make them stop talking. Rachel always shoved me when I did this and said not to be a baby. And then my mom would tell Rachel to be more sensitive.

Moving was a sore subject between us. But I was determined to prove to Rachel and my parents, too, that they could love Applewood Heights as much as I did. I just had to figure out *how*.

I shook off the thought and took a big bite of my raspberry-swirl pancake. "Mmmm-mmm," I said, tasting the sweet and tart raspberry on my tongue. "Should we tell Rachel how good these are?"

"You snooze, you lose," my dad said, helping himself to seconds.

My mom rolled her eyes but didn't disagree.

ᘓ Chapter Two ᘔ

"No one saved me pancakes?" Rachel asked when she finally got up and wandered into the kitchen.

"There's one in the oven," I told her. "Just for you."

"Only one? Gee, thanks."

"You snooze, you lose — right, Dad?" I said.

Rachel rolled her eyes at me. She knew I was right. It's not my fault my pancakes were so popular. Though I suppose it *was* my fault they were delicious.

"It's almost time for my show!" I said, jumping up. I could feel myself getting all excited again and did my ants-in-my-pants hop. "I'm going to get Alice!"

"That's fine, honey," my mom said. "Did you brush your teeth yet?"

I flashed my teeth instead of answering.

"Brush!" she demanded.

I stomped to the bathroom and did as I was told, then poked my head in the kitchen to see how Rachel liked her pancake.

"It's pretty good, but it would have been better with chocolate chips," she said.

"Everything's better with chocolate chips! Obviously. But we didn't have any."

Rachel shrugged and took another bite. "Still pretty good. Nice work."

I gave her a thumbs-up, ran to our room to grab my baking notebook, and headed out with a hop, hop, hop!

At the elevator, I waited for the familiar *DING!* Then I stepped in and sniffed for clues about who rode it last or what they'd been eating. It was a game I liked to play with Alice and Lucas. Sometimes the elevator did not smell great, such as when someone who'd been in there had been extra sweaty or had some stinky take-out food. When that happened, I held my breath or breathed through my mouth. But sometimes the elevator smelled wonderful! We always knew if Mrs. Doolan from 210 had been in there because it smelled like fresh peaches. We didn't know if it was the shampoo she used or her perfume, but it sure smelled good.

Mrs. Doolan was one of my favorite residents at

Applewood Heights. She was always friendly and nice to me, and remembered to ask what I'd been baking, and why I hadn't stopped by with my friends (she meant Alice and Lucas, of course) to share. I never told her the truth, which is that we didn't like knocking on her door because her little dog, Chet, would bark and growl at us as if he wanted *us* for a treat.

Alice thought Chet had rabies, but Lucas said rabid animals don't survive as long as Chet has. Chet was so old, almost all his fur was gray and some of it had even fallen out. Chet was small and wiry, but he was strong. Once, when Mr. Barrett's cat, Gregory, from 201, got out in the hall, Mrs. Doolan had stepped out with Chet on his leash. Chet dashed after Gregory. He pulled on his leash so hard, Mrs. Doolan fell over and Chet tried to drag her down the hall!

I didn't see it happen, but Alice, who lived on the same floor, swore it was a true story. Mrs. Doolan had to have her arm in a sling because she hurt her shoulder when she fell. After that, Gregory must have learned his lesson because he never tried to escape again.

Today the elevator smelled like a cinnamon roll, and that meant Ms. Medina from 503 had been here. She wore stylish suits to work and fancy cologne that smelled sweet and spicy. She had wavy black hair and wore red lipstick. She also had black-and-white wing-tip shoes, which I had never seen before I met her. I complimented her on them once, and she told me what they were called. She got them at the Goodwill shop for three dollars, and they'd never been worn. Ms. Medina knew all the tricks to find the nicest clothes at thrift shops. She found out the days when they put the newly donated things out and made sure to get there as soon as the doors opened so she could have first pick. Sometimes she gave me, Alice, and Lucas fashion advice, even though none of us really cared much about how fancy we looked. Ms. Medina was one more reason I loved living at Applewood Heights. I didn't need fashion advice, but I knew if I ever *did*, I'd have her to help me.

The elevator dinged again, and the door slid open. I took one last big sniff of cinnamon cologne before stepping out. *Mmmmm.* Then I sauntered down the hall to Alice's place.

Before I got to her door, a familiar voice called out, "Ivy!"

I turned and saw Donnalyn, the apartment building's maintenance person, striding toward me. Her big tool belt clanked against her hips with each step.

"Just the person I was looking for!" she said.

Donnalyn often let me tag along and help her make repairs to the apartments. I was becoming a pro at fixing leaky faucets, replacing loose linoleum, repairing window screens, and lots more! In addition to cooking, one of my favorite things was making gadgets and learning how to fix things. At our old house, sometimes my mom and dad told me I was too young to help, or that I would get in the way, or that it was too dangerous, or a million other reasons that kept me from working on my fix-it skills. But at Applewood Heights, there was always something that needed to be done, and Donnalyn was always willing to teach me something new. Only today, Donnalyn would have to wait. It was *Bake It to Make It!* time!

"Can't talk now," I told her. "It's almost time for my show!"

"I wanted to let you know that the soap trick worked on Mr. Barrett's kitchen drawer," Donnalyn said.

Mr. Barrett had been complaining that the wooden drawers in his kitchen wouldn't slide open easily, and since they weren't on metal sliders, we couldn't grease them to make them move smoothly.

"He was pretty impressed you came up with such an easy solution," Donnalyn said.

"I learned from the best," I told her.

"Aw, shucks."

I could tell Donnalyn was only pretending to be embarrassed.

"I gotta go get Alice now," I said. "We can't be late!"

"Have fun, then! And don't forget to come find me if you make something delicious."

"Everything we make is delicious," I said.

"Mostly!" Donnalyn called back as she clomped off in the other direction.

Hmph. No one seemed to be able to forget about the "Beet-Its."

❧ Chapter Three ☙

Alice opened her door before I could even knock.

"Spying again?" I asked.

She slid aside the little stool she'd been standing on to look through the peephole in the door. "I wasn't spying—I was on lookout duty," Alice said.

Alice's apartment was right near the elevator, and she could watch everyone coming and going on her floor. One time I stood on the stool with her, and we took turns spying—I mean, being "on the lookout." As we watched people come and go, Alice told me stories about them. That's how I first learned about Mrs. Doolan and Chet. It was fun to hear interesting stories about the people as they walked by, but then Mrs. Johnson, Alice's grandmother, yelled at us to get down and stop our nonsense.

"Got your notebook?" I asked Alice.

"Of course," she said, flashing her neon-green one at me. "You?"

I held mine up. It was bright blue with a cupcake I had drawn on the cover. I also made a pen holder through the spirals, so I'd always have a pen. You never know when inspiration might strike, and I needed to be ready to write down my ideas.

"We're going to watch our show!" Alice called to her grandma.

"Be good!" a stern voice yelled back.

Mrs. Johnson was kind of old and didn't get out of bed until almost lunchtime. I wasn't sure where Alice's parents were. Alice didn't talk about them, and Rachel said it's not polite to ask personal questions like that. She said if Alice wanted me to know about them, she'd tell me.

One time, though, when Alice's grandma yelled at her for standing on the stool and looking through the peephole (Alice kept doing it no matter how many times her grandma said not to), she made a comment about someone named Stevie and to stop looking for her because it was a big waste of time. A sad look came over Alice's face. Later, when I asked who Stevie was, Alice got very quiet and said, "No one. A ghost." And that was the end of the conversation.

Still, I thought a lot about this Stevie, and why Alice was on the lookout for her, especially because the mention of her made Alice seem so sad and worried.

I knew what it was like to worry, too. Before we came here, my parents argued about money all the time. I worried that maybe they didn't love each other anymore. But when the bank foreclosed on our house and we were all feeling scared about where we would live, my parents promised that no matter what happened, we would always love each other. A house doesn't make a home; people do. That's what Rachel said. I liked that. And now I loved our new home! I just wished my family felt the same way.

"Ms. Medina's been in here," Alice said when we stepped into the elevator.

"Yup," I said, taking another big whiff of the fading cinnamon scent.

"She sure is pretty, huh?" Alice said. "I can't believe she lives in this place."

"What do you mean?" I asked.

Alice shrugged. "I don't know. She seems so fancy. Why's she gotta live here?"

"What's so bad about here?" I didn't like how

this conversation was going. Alice sounded just like Rachel.

"I mean . . . look around you, Ivy. This place is pretty crummy. The carpet's all worn out and stained. The walls are grimy and need to be painted. It's kinda run-down—"

"No, it's not!" I didn't need Alice to point out all the ways that our building wasn't nice. I had Rachel for that. And besides, I didn't care if things were a little run-down—it was the people I liked. Who cared if things weren't picture-perfect? What mattered was the company!

"Well, I'm glad Ms. Medina lives here," I said. "I like her."

"I didn't say I didn't like her." Alice sounded a little huffy, like she was about to tell me off. "But you shouldn't be glad she lives here."

"Why not?" I knew I shouldn't ask, but I couldn't help myself. I was feeling huffy, too.

"Because living here means you failed."

I could not believe my ears. "No, it doesn't!"

"People only live here when they can't afford any-place else to live, so explain that."

"Just because you can't afford something, doesn't

mean you failed! It just means you don't have a lot of money. That's not fair!"

Alice shrugged again, as if it didn't matter either way, which made me even more upset.

"Grandma says people come here because they're down on their luck," Alice continued.

"Luck has nothing to do with it," I said. "I don't like that phrase at all."

The elevator opened to the third floor, and we stepped out. Alice strutted ahead of me, which was her way of telling me she was done with the topic.

I stayed back a minute, watching her hop onto the stains in the hallway carpet. It was a game we'd made up with Lucas. The rule was to hop from spot to spot to see if we could get all the way to the end of the hall by only stepping on the stains. I felt bad watching her do it now, though. It felt like she was making fun of the place.

None of the people who lived here had failed. They hadn't! Maybe some people even felt lucky to be here, like me. Stains and all.

An ache grew in my throat. I wanted to go home, but then Alice turned back and smiled at me.

"C'mon, slowpoke!" she called.

I swallowed down the ache and ran to catch up.

"It's *Bake It to Make It!* time!" Alice sang in a high-pitched voice that sounded like Carly Lin. She wiggled her bum and danced.

I followed her, doing my own happy dance the rest of the way down the hall until we got to Lucas's door.

We heard giggling on the other side, and Alice turned bright red. I felt my cheeks get hot, too. "Guess we're not the only ones keeping lookout," I said, elbowing Alice.

Alice rolled her eyes. "Lucas!" she yelled at the tiny hole in the door. "Open up and let us in before we miss the show!"

Lucas swung open the door and grinned. "Nice moves," he said, laughing.

"You're just jealous because you don't have my style," Alice said.

"I have my own style!" Lucas did a little shuffle with his feet to show us. He danced across the kitchen floor toward the living room. "Come on!"

We copied his moves and followed him inside.

Ꮔ Chapter Four Ꮔ

"Hey, kids!" Lucas's dad greeted us from his fancy blue chair in their living room. It was the kind that leaned way back when you pushed a button on the arm. The chair could also lean you forward to make it easier to get out of. Mr. Stevens had some problems with his legs and used a walker to get around.

Once when Mr. Stevens let us stay home alone while he was at a doctor's appointment, we pretended the chair was a dentist's chair and leaned each other way back in it to give each other cleanings. When Mr. Stevens came home and saw we'd all used the same toothbrush, he was the opposite of happy.

Lucas said it shouldn't matter since we were brushing each other's teeth with toothpaste so the brush was clean. This made perfect sense to me. But Mr. Stevens said he could not believe his ears and sent me and Alice home after making us promise we'd clean our teeth with our own toothbrushes the second we got there. Twice!

As soon as I became friends with Lucas and Alice, I knew we'd always be together. We made plans to share an apartment and open our own restaurant when we grew up. Alice even created a section in her notebook for menu ideas, and Lucas drew designs for the dining-room layout in his. We spent hours discussing the possibilities.

I smiled at the thought and hugged my own notebook to my chest. I loved Saturdays, and I loved my friends. I was the exact opposite of being down on my luck, like Alice said. In fact, I'd never felt luckier!

"Show's about to start!" Mr. Stevens said.

We sat on the floor in front of his chair and waited for *Bake It to Make It!* to come on. We each held our notebooks in our laps, ready to take notes and write down ideas for using whatever Pot-Pourri ingredients would be on the day's show.

I opened my notebook to a clean page and wrote the date in my best handwriting. Then the music for the show began, and we all sang the tune at the top of our lungs. Even Mr. Stevens chimed in.

"Dooooo de doo-doo! It's tiiiiiiime for another week of *Bake It to Make It!* with your judges"—we paused to listen for how the announcer would introduce them—"Carrrly Cupcake and Dusssstin Doughnut!" The announcer always changed the judges' names to have something to do with the daily challenge.

"Just kidding, just kidding," the announcer went on. "Introducing the cupcake queen, Carly Lin, and our debonair doughnut master, Dustin Kendal!"

"Ooh, today's challenge is going to be cupcakes versus doughnuts!" Lucas said.

"I wonder what the ingredients will be," Alice said. "Something weird, I bet."

I inched closer to the screen. "I hope they include chocolate. We haven't had chocolate in a long time!"

Lucas and Alice moved up closer next to me.

"Uh-uh, back up now—you're too close to the screen," Mr. Stevens said. "When I was your age, my grandfather worried if I sat too close to the TV, I'd get radiation poisoning! Can you believe that?"

"Well, you must, since you won't let us sit close," Lucas said.

"Heh. Good point. But you three are blocking my view. Now, get back."

We all slid back toward Mr. Stevens. Lucas leaned

24

against his dad's legs and smiled. Mr. Stevens reached forward and rubbed Lucas's shoulders.

Then the judges revealed the secret Pot-Pourri ingredients: flour, eggs, Brie, and scallions.

"What's Brie?" Lucas asked.

"It's a creamy cheese with a gross white skin on the outside," I told him, proud to know all about it. "But the creamy part tastes pretty good."

"When did you have that?" Alice asked.

"The real estate office where my dad works used to serve fancy food at open-house events to get people to come look at new properties for sale, and he got to bring home leftovers."

"How come they don't do it anymore?"

"I don't know." I realized it had been a long time since my dad had brought home any special treats. "I think it's because fewer people are buying houses these days."

"Is your dad going to lose his job?" Lucas asked in his matter-of-fact way.

I squirmed in my place on the floor. I knew things weren't as great as they had once been, which is why we had to move here. But lose his job? Could he?

"Lucas! Don't ask that!" Alice said.

"Why not?"

"Because it's rude," Mr. Stevens said. "I'm sorry, Ivy. That's none of our business."

"It's all right," I said. I didn't know the answer anyway. But now that Lucas had brought it up, it made me worry. What would happen if my dad lost his job? Would we be able to stay at Applewood Heights? Or would we have to go somewhere for people even more "down on their luck"? Was there such a place?

I pretended to make a note in my notebook so I didn't have to talk about it anymore.

One baking contestant made doughnuts flavored with scallions, which sounded pretty terrible. Another made cupcakes with Brie and scrambled egg inside.

"Oh, brother. Those two are not going to make it," Alice said. "Whoever heard of a scrambled-egg cupcake?"

"They're going savory," I said, glad to be talking about something else. "It's brilliant!" I carefully wrote down all the methods each contestant used to make their concoctions in case any were a hit with the judges.

Then the big timer went off, and the contestants had to stop what they were working on and let the judges inspect and taste what they'd made.

"My money's on the scallion doughnuts," Lucas

said. "Maybe they'll taste like the scallion pancakes Dad and I order from Taste of Beijing."

"Those are top-notch," Mr. Stevens agreed.

I'd had those once before when my mom chose take-out for her birthday dinner. "I bet you're right!" I said.

Carly carefully sniffed the doughnut before taking a bite. Dustin waited for her response before trying one himself.

"Do you think they'd be good dipped in soy sauce, like they give you at Taste of Beijing?" Lucas asked.

"Sounds good to me!" I wrote it down in case we decided to try them. The contestants were allowed to add some minor ingredients to their creations as long as the Pot-Pourri ones were the main feature.

"These are deeeeeeeeelicious!" Carly said.

You could tell if Carly really liked something because she exaggerated certain syllables when she was happy.

The judges tried each contestant's food and then declared the scallion doughnut the winner, which meant that's what we'd be making, too. It was a good thing, because I wasn't sure how we'd ever afford Brie.

"Well, kids, I guess we know what you're making next!" Mr. Stevens said.

"Scallion doughnuts!" we all shouted at the same time.

I quickly drew a doughnut in my notebook and held it up to show Lucas and Alice.

"Ingredient time!" Lucas said, jumping up from the floor.

"Can't wait to try them when you're done!" Mr. Stevens said.

"They will be deeeeeeeeelicious," I said in my best Carly voice.

"I don't doubt it," said Mr. Stevens.

❧ Chapter Five ❧

We started gathering the ingredients at Lucas's, but all he had was flour and one egg. At Alice's, we found another egg, but we still needed scallions and soy sauce, so we went to my apartment.

"Where are Mom and Dad?" I asked Rachel, who was back in bed, reading a book with George.

"They went for a walk. How was the show?"

"Great! We need scallions and soy sauce," I told her.

"Check the fridge, but I don't think we have either."

"We'll ask the neighbors."

"Don't talk to strangers."

Sometimes Rachel was so bossy.

"Neighbors aren't strangers," I said. "Just because *you* haven't gotten to know everyone doesn't mean we haven't. You need to get out more."

Rachel looked offended. "I get out plenty! I'm only watching out for you. That's what big sisters do."

"You talk to Ivy like she's a little kid," Lucas told her.

Rachel put down her book. "She *is* a little kid. And so are you."

Now it was Lucas who looked offended. "Nine is *not* little," he said.

"C'mon," I said, motioning for us to leave. "She's no fun."

"Hey!" Rachel said.

"Well, it's true. You mope around all the time instead of playing."

"Reading isn't moping!"

"Hmph."

Lucas and Alice followed me back to the kitchen. We found an almost-empty bottle of soy sauce in the fridge but no scallions.

"That's not enough for a dipping sauce," Alice pointed out.

"At least it's something!" I said. That was a saying my mom liked to use when we had to make do with what we had. What she meant was, it's better than nothing.

We decided to ask some neighbors for help. Our first stop was at Mrs. Ocasio's on the first floor. We'd asked for help from her before and then shared our final product to thank her. Her favorite was our "Orange Delights." The Pot-Pourri ingredients that day were butter, sugar, flour, and an orange. We'd made shortbread cookies and used zest from the orange to flavor them.

"I bet you're looking for scallions," Mrs. Ocasio said when she opened the door. "I don't have any of those, but I do have some margarine. That was a great show today, wasn't it? Made me crave some doughnuts. I bet orange ones would be delicious!"

I jotted a note about orange doughnuts. Not a bad idea!

"We have enough butter," Alice told her. "But thanks."

"If you make the doughnuts, I'll be happy to taste test them for you!" Mrs. Ocasio said.

I added her name in my notebook under "Scallion Doughnut Taste Volunteers."

"And, Ivy," Mrs. Ocasio said. "Before you go, I need a light bulb changed in my bedroom. Donnalyn hasn't been by to help. Would you mind? There's a step stool and a box of bulbs in the hallway closet."

"Sure thing!" I said.

"You're a lifesaver," Mrs. Ocasio said when I was all done.

That made my whole body beam. I love being helpful!

"You sure like fixing things," Lucas said as we walked back to the elevator.

"What's wrong with that?" I asked.

"Nothing. It's just different."

"I like being different," I said. "Think how boring it would be if we were all the same."

We visited four more neighbors' apartments in search of ingredients but didn't have any luck, so we went back to my place to ask Rachel for help.

"Why do you need scallions and soy sauce, anyway?" she asked. "You usually make something sweet."

"We need to make scallion doughnuts," Lucas told her.

Rachel made a yucky face. "That sounds gross."

"Carly Lin liked them," Alice said.

Rachel rolled her eyes and went to the bureau, where she kept a sock stuffed with the money she saved from her summer job taking care of the farm animals who lived across the street from our old house.

"How much do scallions cost?" she asked, reaching around in the messy drawer.

"How should I know?" I asked. It was a little

ungrateful of me, since she was offering to buy them for us when we hadn't even asked.

"We need more soy sauce, too," Lucas said.

Rachel gave me a five-dollar bill. "Hopefully this is enough. If they're good, share with me. And stay together on your walk, and remember not to talk to strangers."

"We're not five," Lucas said, annoyed. "And why are you so afraid of strangers?"

"I'm not afraid. I want you to be safe."

"We always are!" Alice said cheerfully. "And we've gone alone before, you know. Lots of times. We'll be fine!"

"OK, OK. Sorry for caring," Rachel said.

"Bye-eee!" I said, and gave her a hug. "And thank you!"

Rachel resisted at first, but then hugged back. Rachel often seemed grumpy, but deep down she loved me a lot and did nice things, like give me money for scallions even though she didn't like them. I was lucky to have a sister like her.

Out in the hallway, Becka Yee and her mom, Tracy, were getting off the elevator.

"Hey, Becka!" I called to her. "Wanna cook with us?"

Even though Becka was a year older, she sometimes

liked to play with us. As we walked closer, I could see Becka was crying.

"What's wrong?" Alice asked.

Tracy hugged Becka to her side. "Hi, kids." Tracy looked really happy, which seemed strange in contrast to poor Becka. "We're moving! My temporary job turned permanent and I got a raise!"

My heart sank a little, and right away I felt guilty. It was good news! But I was sad that Becka was going to leave.

People moved out of the apartments a lot. Sometimes they seemed glad about moving, but not always. Mr. Stevens said people moved in and out of here so often, the building should have a revolving door. A lot of families came for a short time until they "got back on their feet," as my dad said. I didn't really understand that phrase. It made it sound like people here were sitting around, trying to stand up. But everyone here worked really hard all the time and hardly had a chance to sit down at all, unless they were like Mr. Stevens and had a physical challenge.

"Where will you go?" Lucas asked Tracy.

"Clover Hill Apartments over on the north side of town. The apartment is a bit bigger, and the building has a community garden!"

"That sounds nice," Alice said.

Becka wiped her face with the back of her hand, but tears kept slipping down her cheeks anyway.

"Sorry, Becka," I said. "We can come visit you, though!"

"We'd love that," Tracy said. "Maybe you can bring us one of your great food creations. Or you can make something with the veggies from our garden!"

Tracy was so nice. When I first met her, I called her Ms. Yee, and she laughed and said, "That's my mom. Call me Tracy!" I was going to miss her.

"That sounds fun!" I told her. "We'll have a picnic!"

Becka smiled, but it seemed like it hurt to do it.

"It'll be great, Becka," Alice said. "I bet it's a lot nicer than this place."

"I don't care if it's nicer. I like it here."

"Me too," I said. I was about to tell her how Rachel and my parents also wanted to move, but Alice nudged me, which meant to be quiet.

Tracy smiled uncomfortably and pulled Becka to her side again to give her a little hug.

We all stood and stared at the worn rug in the hall, not sure what else to say.

"Where are you all headed, anyway?" Tracy asked, breaking up the awkward moment.

"We need to get some ingredients for today's *Bake It to Make It!* challenge," I said.

"You wanna go with them, honey?" Tracy asked Becka.

Becka shook her head and leaned in closer against her mom.

I felt so sad for her. I knew what it was like to move away from the home you love and to feel scared about what the new place would be like.

I reached out to touch her shoulder, but I couldn't think of something to say that would make her feel better.

"Thanks, kids," Tracy said as she led Becka away.

We waited for the elevator in silence. I felt a familiar tug in my tummy. Whenever I got sad, instead of crying, I'd start to feel queasy, as if I might throw up. I called it my sad stomach feeling. I'm not sure when it started happening, but probably around the time my parents began arguing about money, back when we still lived at the farmhouse. Sometimes at night I could hear them downstairs when they thought Rachel and I were asleep. On those nights, I would tiptoe quietly into Rachel's room and crawl into bed with her. She didn't like it when our parents fought, either. She'd whisper stories to me to try to distract us from what was happening downstairs. But sometimes the worry still found its way into my tummy.

On those nights, I'd snuggled closer to Rachel, and she'd rub my back and hum some song or another to help me fall asleep.

I rubbed my tummy, feeling the familiar ache, and thought about Rachel still being sad about leaving our old home and hoped Becka wouldn't feel that way at her new apartment for so long.

"We are definitely going to visit her," I said. "Right?"

"How?" Alice asked. "They'll be so far away."

"I don't know. Maybe my mom can drive us."

"Becka will make new friends," Lucas said. "She won't need us."

"I'll always need you," I said. "You're the greatest friends I've ever had!"

Alice and Lucas looked at each other, then at me, as if they knew something I didn't. As if they felt sorry for me for not knowing whatever it was.

"What?" I asked. I did not like that look one bit. It made me feel scared, like something bad was about to happen.

Alice took my hand and squeezed it. "Don't worry. We aren't going anywhere," she said. "Except shopping!"

ও Chapter Six ৩

"First one to find the scallions gets first bite of the doughnuts!" Lucas said the minute we got to the market. He raced toward the vegetable section with Alice at his heels. I was sure there was a no-running-in-the-store rule, so I walked as fast as I could without technically running. I was not a rule-breaker!

There were so many fresh greens along the refrigerated wall, we weren't sure where to start our search. Lucas called out each label as he scanned the shelves. "Bok choy! Mustard greens! Kale!"

Brandi, the store manager, came over to help. She was our favorite and always offered us a free apple or some other kind of fruit from the sale bin when we came by.

"Something's wrong with this picture," she said. "Why are you shopping for vegetables? I usually only find you three in the baking section."

"We need scallions," Lucas explained.

"Oh, yeah?"

"To make scallion doughnuts," I said. "Like pancakes but not."

"Oooh, I love scallion pancakes. I'm not sure about doughnuts, though." She walked over to a section of green stuff and pulled out a small bunch of scallions held together with a red rubber band. "Here you go."

"We were hoping to try soy sauce to dip the doughnuts in," Alice said. "You sell that here, too, right?"

"Actually, there are a bunch of packets in the staff fridge out back. No one ever uses all the soy sauce that comes with takeout. Let me see what I can find for you."

She came back carrying a fistful of packets.

"Wow!" Lucas said. "Are these for free?"

"Sure!" Brandi said. "Let me know how the doughnuts turn out!"

Back at my apartment, we decided to bake instead of fry since we didn't want to waste a lot of oil. The only problem was, we didn't have a doughnut mold to bake the batter in. But I had an idea!

I shaped some tinfoil into tiny balls and put one in the center of each cup in a muffin tin.

"Here," I said to Alice. "Hold this down while I pour batter in, and the batter will go around the foil to make a hole in the doughnut."

She pressed her finger on a foil ball while I poured the thick batter into one of the cups.

"But now I can't take my finger off or the tinfoil will float to the top!" Alice said.

Rats. Hadn't thought of that.

"We'll have to put something heavy on top, but it has to be something that will be safe in the oven," Lucas said.

I quickly rummaged through the cupboard and pulled out an assortment of coffee mugs, which I filled halfway with water. "If we slip these on top of each ball, I think it'll hold them down."

"But we won't be able to see the dough to know when it's ready to come out," Lucas pointed out.

"We'll have to trust our instincts." I slipped the first mug over the foil Alice was still pressing her finger on. "Well?"

"No way to tell," Lucas said.

"It'll work," I said. "I'm sure of it."

"But how do you know?" Alice asked.

"Have I ever steered you wrong?"

"I'm sure we could think of a time," Lucas answered.

I was, too. But I wasn't going to remind them of any! I nudged him. "What other choice do we have? Let's try it."

We filled the rest of the muffin cups using the same method, then carefully lifted the heavy tray and put it in the oven.

We sat on the kitchen floor and watched through the glass window as our concoction baked. Every so often, one of us would sniff the air.

"Hint of onion," I said when it was almost time to take them out.

"Essence of doughnut," Lucas said.

Finally, we all agreed the dough must be cooked by now. I put on my oven mitts and carefully lifted the tray out and set it on top of the stove. Then I slowly lifted one of the mugs up with my bulky mitts. The tiny doughnut underneath looked like a moldy Cheerio.

"Well, maybe the others will look better," I said. We moved all the mugs and turned the doughnuts onto a cooling rack. Some of them looked like squashed Cheerios because the dough had spread under the foil, despite our efforts.

"Those ones look like mini scallion muffins!" Lucas said.

Rachel came in to see how things were going.

"Hmm," she said, leaning closer to inspect them. "Huh."

"What do you mean by that 'huh'?" I asked.

"Smells good? I mean . . . looks aren't everything, right?" She winked at me. Rachel wasn't *always* grumpy. "When do I get to try one?" she asked.

"They need to cool a bit more," Alice said. "And you can't have a whole one because we have other taste testers to share with."

"Sheesh, shouldn't family members get first dibs?"

"Donors get first dibs!" Lucas said.

"I'm the one who paid for the scallions!"

"Oh, right. Fine. You can have a whole one."

We all stood around to watch the doughnuts cool.

"Becka Yee is moving," I told Rachel. "Her mom got a new job."

"That's great! Tracy is so nice. I'm happy for her."

"It's not great for us," I said. "We like Becka. And now we'll never see her."

Rachel frowned at me. "But it's great for Becka, Ivy. And her mom."

"I know, I know."

I did know. So why did I feel so crummy about it?

"I hope we never move," I said. "I love it here."

"Me too!" Lucas said.

Alice didn't answer. Neither did Rachel.

I knew Rachel's feelings on the matter, but Alice? I'd been sure Alice would always want to stay here with me and Lucas.

"You don't want to move, do you, Alice?" I asked.

"Only under certain circumstances," she said quietly.

"Like what?" I asked.

"I don't want to talk about it."

I wondered if the circumstances had anything to do with the mysterious Stevie. But if Alice said she didn't want to talk about it, I knew better than to ask. Still, that didn't stop me from thinking about it. I couldn't imagine life here without Alice or Lucas—that part was one thing I *didn't* want to think about.

When the doughnuts cooled off, we cut one up in thirds and each dipped a piece in the bowl we'd emptied all the soy sauce packets into. We chewed quietly and waited until we all swallowed before sharing notes, like the judges did on *Bake It to Make It!*

"A note of onion," Alice said.

"The soy sauce is very salty," Lucas added. "I think we should've added some brown sugar to it."

"We have that!" I got a bag out from the cupboard and stirred a small spoonful into the bowl until it dissolved. Then we all tried again.

"Mmm. I do declare this is the perfect dipping sauce," Alice said, imitating Dustin Kendal.

"The sweetness from the sugar adds a nice balance," Lucas added.

We all turned to Rachel and slid a doughnut her way. She dipped it in the sauce and took a nibble. Then dipped again.

We all scoffed at the same time.

"What?" she asked.

"Double dipping? What a rookie," I said. "You could've at least cut your piece in two so you didn't put your bitten end in the sauce. How gauche."

"This from the kid who shared a toothbrush with her friends? And how do you even know what 'gauche' means?"

I rolled my eyes and shook my head disappointedly. "Sharing is different with friends."

"I'm your *sister*!"

"Never mind," Alice said, changing the subject. "Do you like it?"

"It's fine," Rachel said, triple dipping.

"Rachel!" I yelled.

She smirked. "I like the sauce. Nice work. But next time, I'd make them pancakes."

ℭ Chapter Seven ℘

On Becka and Tracy's moving day, Alice, Lucas, and I helped them carry boxes down to a big truck. Lots of other people from the building joined in to help, too. Lugging the boxes made me think of when my family had to move last summer. Because the old farmhouse was so much bigger than the apartment, we had to leave a lot of things behind. My parents had a yard sale, and Rachel and I had to go through all of our stuff to decide what to keep and what to sell or give away. Some things were easy to let go of, like old toys I'd outgrown and didn't play with anymore. But others were harder to say goodbye to, such as a bunch of stuffed animals I'd had since I was a baby. But it was hardest for my parents, who had to leave behind furniture that once belonged to my grandparents and held special memories. "They're only objects," my mom kept saying. "These things don't really hold memories; we do." But I could tell she said it more to convince herself than me and Rachel. And by the way she still touched the table from our old place with such tenderness, I knew she was feeling its memories.

Before we knew it, Becka and Tracy's apartment was empty, and the truck was jam-packed with furniture and boxes. All the kids from the building moped around, not wanting to say goodbye.

Rachel nudged me to go over and give Becka a hug.

"I'll miss you," I told her. There was a hard lump in the back of my throat that ached when I said it.

"You can come visit," Becka said. She seemed to be in a much better mood than the day her mom had told us about the move.

"My new room has a closet!" Becka said.

"That's great!" I said. "I had a closet at my old house, but I didn't have too many clothes to put in it, so I turned it into a clubhouse."

"Ooh!" Becka said. "I want to do that!"

I didn't tell her that George was the only other club member besides my stuffed animals, and that it wasn't much fun. I didn't miss having a closet at all! At our apartment, Rachel and I have to share a tiny bureau for our clothes, and most don't fit, so we have to keep the rest in plastic bins under our beds. Rachel says our room is way too cramped, but I think it's cozy.

"My mom says I can have a sleepover party," Becka said. "As soon as we're settled in."

"Can I come?" I asked.

"Of course! I wouldn't have brought it up if I didn't want you to come."

That made me feel better. I gave Becka my tightest hug to show her how much I cared. But she got squirmy, as if she didn't want me to hang on quite so long, so I had to let go.

"I'm glad you're happy," I said.

"Thanks, Ivy." Becka joined her mom in the cab of the truck.

All of us kids waved and ran after them as Tracy and Becka drove out of the parking lot. Tracy beeped the horn when they turned onto the main road.

"Well, that's the last we'll see of her," Lucas said.

"No, it isn't!" I argued. "She invited us to come visit. She said I could come to her sleepover!"

"That's what they all say," Lucas said. "But once they leave, they forget about us."

"I don't believe you," I said. My stomach began to

feel funny, and I was sure a case of sad stomach was coming on.

"C'mon," Lucas said, heading back toward the building.

But I didn't want to go back inside. "I'm not going in," I said. I walked over to one of the benches near the entrance of the building.

Alice plopped down next to me.

"I hope I never have to move again," I told her. "But if I do, I'll come back to visit you. And I'll invite you for a sleepover and mean it. I swear."

Alice shrugged. "What do you mean, 'if'? Seems like almost everyone moves from here eventually."

"Don't say that!" Alice's words made my stomach hurt even more.

"OK," Alice said. "Take it easy."

We watched Lucas go inside.

I pressed my hand to my aching belly and rubbed it, but it didn't feel better.

"Do you think you'll move, too?" I asked.

A curtain of sadness crossed over Alice's face. "My grandma has no plans to move. But if . . ." Alice trailed off, like whatever she was imagining was too much to hope for.

"If what?"

She shrugged a little again. "Never mind. Grandma says I need to let it go."

"You mean Stevie coming back?" I thought again about Alice on the lookout, waiting.

"How do you know about her?"

"I don't. But . . . I heard your grandma mention the name. And I remember you called her a ghost one time. But if she's a ghost, does that mean . . . she died? But you look for her, don't you? Through the peephole?"

Alice got all quiet, and the sadness curtain seemed even thicker.

"That's my mom," Alice said. "Stevie. And she didn't die."

"Why did you call her a ghost, then?"

Alice looked down at her sandals. They were red flip-flops and had little ladybugs on the straps. "I don't know. I guess because sometimes that's how she feels to me. I can see her in my mind, but I can't touch her. You know, like a memory or a dream. We don't know where she is. My grandma says for all she knows, Stevie's dead and gone. I bet that's the only way my grandma would forgive Stevie, anyway, for leaving the way she did. But I don't believe it. I know she's out there, and she's coming back for me. Someday."

"Why did she leave?"

Alice huffed. "I don't like to talk about it. She just did. OK?"

I knew I shouldn't keep asking, but I couldn't help myself. "What do you think happened to her?"

"I don't know. I haven't seen her for a long time. When she brought me here, she told me we were visiting. But the next morning when I woke up on the fold-out couch in Grandma's living room, my mom and all her stuff were gone. She didn't even leave a note."

I could not imagine my mom leaving us that way. It hurt too much to even try.

"Do you . . . have a dad?"

"Everyone has a dad."

"I know, but—"

"I never met him." Alice's voice had an annoyed tone in it. Sometimes she used it when Lucas and I didn't agree with her about something, like how to cook the weekly *Bake It to Make It!* challenge.

"My mom has a drug problem, OK? Grandma says she likes to live wild and free and can't be tied down. And drugs make it even worse."

"Oh," I said. I hadn't known someone with a drug problem before. "Sorry."

"Maybe it's my fault she left. Maybe she didn't want

to be tied down, having to take care of me. If she comes back, I'll show her I can take care of myself! I can bake for her and everything! I know I can make things better than they were. I just need a chance to show her."

"I'm sure she didn't leave because of you," I said.

But Alice looked like she didn't believe me.

"My grandma says, when you love something, you have to set it free, even if you're afraid it won't come back. But if it does come back, it was meant to be. Or . . . you were meant to be together. Something like that. I guess she stopped trying to find Stevie because she had to let her be free and see if she'd come back. Grandma never talks with me about Stevie's problem. She thinks I don't know what it is. When she mentions Stevie, she says she was like a caged bird who only wanted to fly. Grandma says that if Stevie comes back, it means it was meant to be. If she doesn't . . ." Alice trailed off again, but I could guess her next thought. That they weren't meant to be together. I couldn't imagine that was true. I couldn't imagine worrying about it every day, either, looking through the peephole in the door and hoping I'd see my mom coming down the hall.

Alice looked up at the sky and squinted, as if she might see her mom flying freely above us. "I know my mom loves me. She just couldn't take care of me. But like I said, I can take care of myself now. I just need a chance to show her." She seemed to shake off the sadness curtain then, wiggling her body as if she could feel it all over and she had to get it off. "Let's go visit George," she said.

"OK." I stood and wiggled, too, but my sad stomach stayed put. I thought about what it must be like to wonder where your mom was, or why she left without even saying goodbye, or why she hadn't come back. And worse, to wonder if she was safe or even alive.

Rachel told me that when people are addicted to drugs, they can't always take care of other people very well. Sometimes they can't even really take care of themselves. Maybe Stevie left Alice *because* she loved her. Maybe she knew Alice would be safe and well cared for here, with her grandmother.

I decided to keep that thought to myself, though, because Alice was already walking fast ahead of me.

"Wait up!" I called after her.

But Alice just kept walking.

ও Chapter Eight ৩

Alice and I could hear a commotion going on inside the apartment before we even opened the door.

"Can you believe it? Can you believe it?" my mom was yelling.

We hurried in to find my family dancing and jumping up and down in the kitchen.

"What's going on?" I demanded.

"Mom got her old job back!" Rachel grabbed my hands and twirled me in a circle. "It's just part-time, but it's her old library job at the school!"

I hugged my mom, and she squeezed back so tight, I could hardly breathe. Then she let go and did a silly dance that looked a lot like my happy dance. I couldn't remember the last time I saw her look so full of joy.

When I turned to Alice to invite her to join in the fun, though, she did not seem happy at all.

"What's wrong?" I asked.

She looked around, as if searching for something. "Where's George? You said we could visit him."

"I don't know, probably in my room."

She wandered off to find him.

"What's her prob—" Rachel started to ask. And then, "Oh."

"What?"

"C'mon," Rachel said, leading me into the living room.

"Alice probably thinks we're going to move now," Rachel whispered, out of earshot of my parents.

I thought about Tracy and Becka, and how they'd moved because Tracy got a better job. "But *we* won't move, right?" I whispered back.

Rachel twisted her mouth into a one-sided frown. It was a face she made when it seemed like she couldn't think of how to answer one of my questions, which was a lot because I was always stumping her with complicated ones.

My familiar sad stomach feeling gripped my insides.

"I don't want to move!" I said. "Not ever!"

"Shhh! Don't spoil Mom and Dad's celebration. Listen, Ivy. Just because you love it here doesn't mean me, Mom, and Dad do."

I could feel myself getting all worked up. But unlike having happy, excited ants in my pants, it felt as if an angry swarm of bees was thumping inside my chest, trying to get out.

"Why do you all hate it here so much? It's not fair!"

"Don't get upset," Rachel said. "Alice will hear you."

"Alice doesn't care! She doesn't want us to move, either!"

"This is a small apartment," Rachel said. "Too small. Don't you remember what it was like to have a back-yard? And a garden? And a driveway to ride bikes in?"

"What good was that when I didn't have any friends to play with me?"

"You had friends to play with."

"Hardly ever! Before, we had to make silly 'play-dates' and arrange for our parents to drive us to each other's houses, and it was always a big pain because Dad needed the van for work and I couldn't get a ride. Mostly I only had you and Micah. It was lonely and no fun! Now if I want to see my friends, I can hop in the elevator!"

"You! You! You!" Rachel said. "What about other people's happiness?"

Warm teardrops slipped down my face. "You are so mean, Rachel!"

"Why, because I tell the truth?"

My fingers curled into a fist. I wanted to punch Rachel and make her cry, too. Even though we had moved, she could still see Micah when she wanted. She didn't understand why it was different for me. She was the one who cared about herself. She didn't care about me at all! I glared at her and stomped to our room.

Inside, I found Alice holding George and crying, too. Then I felt even worse. I wiped my own tears away and sat next to Alice.

"Just because my mom got a job doesn't mean we're moving," I told her, trying to sound grown up, like Rachel.

"You will, though, eventually." Alice touched her forehead to George's. He purred and tried to lick her nose.

"Don't say that. Maybe my family will grow to love it here and not want to move."

Alice looked doubtful. "Why do you like it here so much, Ivy?"

"Because I have you! And Lucas! And Donnalyn! And everyone else. I'm never lonely, and there's always something fun to do. I belong here."

"You're the only person I know who doesn't want to live someplace nicer."

"I'm not like other people, in case you didn't notice."

"Oh, I noticed." Alice laughed a little.

"Besides, Becka didn't want to leave, either, remember?" I asked.

"Not at first, but look how fast she changed her mind."

"Well, I won't. I know I won't. Not as long as I have you and Lucas. I would never want to leave you! We'll be friends forever!"

George squirmed out of Alice's lap.

"I'm glad you're different," Alice said. "It's what makes you *you*!"

I got up and did my goofy happy dance, wiggling my bum extra fast. "That's why we'll be friends forever. Birds of a feather stick together!" I don't remember where I heard that saying, but it made me feel good. I wiggled my bum again to make Alice laugh, and she got up to join me.

"That's the way!" I said.

George meowed at me.

"I have an idea! Let's make a suit for George!" I said.

George looked at me suspiciously. He did that a lot.

"We can have a cooking contest and dress him up to look like a judge!"

"Ooh," Alice said. "Can we make him a costume to look like Dustin Kendal?"

"Yeah!"

I got the little sewing box my mom gave me for Christmas last year out from under my bed. I kept scraps of cloth in it from clothes I'd outgrown that were too worn to give away. I used the fabric to make little quilts and clothes for the old dollhouse family Rachel handed down to me. I loved how each scrap brought back a memory from the time I wore the clothing it came from. As we pulled the scraps out and decided which ones to use for George's vest, I shared some of these memories with Alice. Then I showed her how to thread a needle and make tiny stitches. Soon we had a spiffy vest and a little hat with holes for George's ears.

"You're my best friend," Alice said. She poked her fingers through the holes to make sure they were big enough for George's pointy ears to fit through.

Her words made me feel all warm and happy inside.

"You're mine," I told her back. In that moment, I knew I'd found my special best friend, like Micah was to Rachel.

George walked between us and sniffed his new clothes. Alice slipped his hat on, but he quickly shook it off and dashed under Rachel's bed, hiding behind her neatly lined-up storage boxes.

"Oh, George," Alice said. "But you looked so cute!" She put the little hat on her own head, but it only settled on the very top because it was so small. "I declare," she said in Dustin's voice. "That cat has no taste, I say, no taste what-so-ever."

I giggled so hard, I almost peed my pants.

"I guess we'll have to give these to Mr. Barrett's cat instead," Alice said.

"They'll look good on Gregory," I agreed. "Too bad, George. You could have been famous."

"Gregory will make a good Dustin," Alice said. "Let's go find him!"

We left George under the bed and raced back to the kitchen.

"What do you have there?" my dad asked.

"We made an outfit for George, but he doesn't like it, so we're going to give it to Gregory."

"Don't go bothering Mr. Barrett, girls. He doesn't seem to like too much excitement."

"Neither does Gregory," Alice pointed out. "But I think he'll appreciate his new outfit. It's purrrrfect!"

"Where's George?" Rachel asked.

"He's hiding under your bed."

"Smart cat. There's a reason cats don't wear clothes, ya know."

"Yes, I know," I said. "It's because no one ever thought to make them properly. Until now!"

I swung my arm around Alice, and we sauntered out of the apartment side by side, doing our special dance as we went. Some people just didn't appreciate our sense of humor. Their loss!

ɕ Chapter Nine ɕ

"I'm hot!" I proclaimed one Monday morning after Rachel and my dad had left for work.

"And it's going to get hotter!" my mom said. Her job at the school hadn't started yet, and she hadn't been called in at the temporary agency where she worked sometimes. It was just us and George, sweating in the apartment and feeling bored.

"Can we go to the pool?" I asked her. "We can take Alice and Lucas!"

"Oh, I don't know, honey. I think it's too hot even for the pool."

My mom never swims at the pool. Instead, she finds a shady spot to sit in a lounge chair and read.

"*Please?* You could swim with us!"

"I don't really have a nice swimsuit to wear."

"You could swim in your shorts!"

She frowned. "No one else does that."

"Aw, who cares what other people do?" I could tell from the look she gave me that my mom cared, and I felt bad for saying it.

"What if Alice, Lucas, and I went on our own? You could stay here. We'd be really careful and not talk to strangers or anything."

"I don't think that's a good idea. Why don't you wait for Rachel to get back, and she can take you?"

"But she won't be back for ages!"

"Read a book. Or go play with Alice for a bit. Or find Donnalyn! She's always happy to have your help. Rachel will be home soon enough."

I hung my head and went to the kitchen to get something for breakfast. It was too hot to heat any-thing up, so I found some cereal and ate it dry out of the box.

"Ivy, are you really putting your hands in that box over and over?" my mom asked, suddenly standing in the doorway.

"It's not the same as double dipping since no one else eats this stuff anyway," I told her.

My mom shook her head. "You know what? I

changed my mind. You're right. It's too hot to do anything but find some cold water." She kissed the top of
my head, which made me smile.

"Yay!" I hugged her and raced to my room to find
my bathing suit. "I'll go tell Alice and Lucas!"

I rapped on Alice's door excitedly. "Pool day!" I yelled
when Alice opened up and stepped back to let me in.

"Hi," she said quietly.

"What's wrong?"

"Is that Ivy?" a voice called from the other room.

"Hi, Mrs. Johnson! Can Alice go to the pool? My
mom can take us."

"Ask her!" Mrs. Johnson called back. Sometimes
Mrs. Johnson was kind of gruff, but she didn't mean
any harm.

"Do you want to go swimming with me?" I asked
Alice.

She looked down at her bare feet. "I guess so."

"Are you all right? You seem sad."

Alice took my arm and led me out into the hallway.

"I think something happened to Stevie," she whispered.

"Why do you think that?"

"I think she called here. I'm not sure. Grandma got all weird when she answered the phone and then hung up when she noticed me listening."

"Why do you think it was Stevie?"

"Because Grandma started crying when she hung up. She only ever cries when it comes to Stevie." Alice's own eyes started to water.

"Did you ask if it was her?"

"Yes. She shook her head and told me not to ask again."

I wasn't sure what to say. Why couldn't her grandma tell her what happened? Sometimes my parents didn't tell me what was going on, and it made me so mad. I don't like secrets!

"What if Stevie was asking to come back?" Alice said. "What if my grandma said no? What if Stevie thinks we don't love her anymore?"

"Alice!" Mrs. Johnson called from inside the apartment. "Are you going swimming or not?"

Even though Alice's grandmother was grumpy now and then, I had never heard her sound like this.

"She always gets mean when she's worried," Alice said, sounding worried, too.

"Alice!" Mrs. Johnson called again.

"Yes! I'm going!" Alice turned to me. "Go get Lucas and come back for me?"

"OK!" I bumped my hip against hers the special way we did to try to cheer each other up, but Alice didn't bump back.

At Lucas's apartment, Mr. Stevens called out for me to come in. He was sitting in his special chair, watching the news.

"I came to invite Lucas to go swimming," I said. "You could come, too!"

Mr. Stevens waved his hand to dismiss the idea. "I can't walk that far," he said.

The public pool was only a few blocks away, but I realized that even walking to the kitchen took a lot of effort for him. I felt bad for not thinking about how hard it would be to walk all the way to the pool.

When Lucas was ready, he gave his dad a big, long hug before he left.

"I wish we had a scooter," Lucas said when we were out in the hallway. "Then my dad could come with us."

"You mean like those little carts they have at the supermarket? I wonder how much those cost."

"Too much," Lucas said. "We've been on a waiting

list for a year and a half to get one from a place that donates them. But since he can walk a little bit, we aren't high on the list, and people who need them more get first dibs."

"That's too bad," I said. "But I guess it's best if they go to people who can't walk first."

"Yeah, I know."

"Maybe we could *make* him a chair! We could put wheels on a regular chair and push him. Or we could find an office chair that already has wheels. I could ask Donnalyn if she has anything like that. Sometimes people leave things behind when they move, and she takes anything she thinks could benefit others who move in. You should see her workshop! It's full of stuff like that."

"I doubt it," Lucas said. "Besides, I don't think my dad would like to be pushed around."

"Why are you giving up so fast? We could at least *try*." I promised myself the next time I saw Donnalyn, I would ask if she had any office chairs.

Alice was standing by the elevator when we got to her floor, so she got in and we all went to my place to find my mom.

"What's up with you?" Lucas asked Alice as the elevator slowly climbed up to the fourth floor.

"Nothing," Alice said, fidgeting with her towel.

"You look like you've been crying," Lucas pointed out.

"I don't want to talk about it." She turned away so we couldn't see her face.

Lucas adjusted his own towel, which hung unevenly over his shoulders. "Sorry."

I couldn't stop thinking about what Alice had said earlier, about Stevie maybe wanting to come back. I wondered what it must feel like for Alice, standing up on that stool every day, watching for her. I reached over and gave Alice's shoulder a squeeze in a reassuring way, but Alice's shoulder felt stiff, like she wanted me to let go.

"I'm fine," Alice said.

The elevator door opened.

"I only want to help," I said.

"Well, since you know there's nothing you can do, I would like you to drop it."

"Sorry."

"Who put a bee in your bonnet?" Lucas asked.

Alice glared at him. "The two of you need to get off my case right now."

Lucas stepped back. "Yeesh! Sor-ry!"

"We're just trying to be good friends," I said. "Because we care about you."

"I know that," Alice said. She reached over and took my sweaty hand for a moment, then let go. "I know."

❧ Chapter Ten ❧

We followed my mom down the hot sidewalk, our flip-flops making a sticky sound against our sweaty feet. *Slap, slap, slap.*

"The water is going to feel sooooooo good," Lucas said.

I thought about the pool water and how the chlorine made my eyes sting. At the lake near our old house, the water was cool and clean with no chemicals. I bet if Lucas thought the pool water felt good, he would *love* the lake water!

"Mom, do you think we could go to our old beach again sometime?" I asked. "I want to take Lucas and Alice."

"Of course," my mom said. "I'll drive your dad to work one morning so we can have the van. That would be fun."

"Doesn't he need the van to take people to see houses?" I asked.

My mom hesitated before she answered. "Some days are slow, and he doesn't have any appointments," she finally said. "We could choose one of those days."

"Right!" I said. It seemed like it had been ages since my dad had sold a house, and I felt bad for reminding my mom about it.

As we walked along, everyone was more quiet than usual. Alice's sad mood seemed to be spreading through each of us. Or maybe it was my fault. I'd made Lucas think about his dad being stuck at home. And I'd made my mom start worrying about my dad's job again. What a crummy way to start out what was supposed to be a fun time.

When we got to the pool, it was packed with kids of all ages. There weren't any chairs left, so we had to hang our towels over the chain-link fence that went around the pool area. We kicked off our flip-flops into a pile.

"You all go in and I'll stay with your things," my mom said.

"But you'll melt!" I told her. "C'mon. No one's gonna take our stuff."

"Don't worry, I'll join you in a bit."

We walked to the edge of the pool and looked down at the water.

"Remember, if you pee in there, the water will turn purple and everyone will know," Lucas said. "And the lifeguard will make you get out, and you'll be banned from swimming here ever again."

"You bring this up every time we come swimming," Alice said. "You know it's not true."

"It could be," Lucas said. "I'm not willing to risk it. And you shouldn't be, either."

"Well, I wouldn't anyway because peeing in the water is gross! Besides," Alice added, "that pee story is an urban legend."

"A what?" I asked.

"It's something people make up to scare you so you won't pee in the water."

"But I bet there's a lot of pee in there," I said. "Look at all those little kids. That one's even wearing a swim diaper!"

"Yuck!" Lucas said. "Are you sure we should go in?"

Alice leaned over the water and sniffed. "Smell all that chlorine? There's enough in there to kill any germs." She stepped into the air over the water and dropped in, going all the way under, then popped up and wiped her wet hair away from her face. "Not very refreshing," she said. "Kind of warm."

"From all the pee?" I joked.

"If it was pee, the water would be purple!" Lucas giggled and jumped in.

I plopped in after him, and we all bobbed around, wading in the warm water. There were so many people in the pool, it wasn't possible to swim around or do much else. Parents and babysitters on the side of the pool kept yelling at their kids to stop splashing. Kids shouted at each other to get out of the way so they could jump in. The lifeguard kept blowing her whistle and ordering people to stop breaking the rules.

"This isn't much fun," I said.

I wished we were at the beach I used to ride my bike to with Rachel and Micah. Even though I hardly ever had friends to play with there, at least it was never crowded like this. And Rachel and Micah always made a point of playing with me.

Thinking about those fun days, I realized why Rachel missed our old home so much. Now she was the one who seemed lonely instead of me. And I remembered how that felt.

Alice twirled in the water. Lucas copied her.

"Well," Lucas said, "it may be crowded, but it's better than being stuck in a hot apartment."

"Next time, let's get a ride to the beach with my mom," I said. "I think you two would like it a lot more."

"Doesn't the beach have frogs and other stuff in the water?" Lucas asked.

"Yeah, but so what?"

"Do they pee in the water?"

"Of course! And fish poop in it. But it doesn't matter."

Alice shuddered. "Now *that's* gross!"

"Haven't you two ever gone swimming in a lake before?" I asked. "It's not gross. It's clean! You can see the sandy bottom and everything!"

"I prefer the pool," Lucas said. "At least there's chlorine in here to kill the germs."

"You don't know what you're missing," I said.

Alice rolled her eyes. "You sound like such a snob, Ivy. Talking about how much better things were where you used to live."

"Yeah," Lucas agreed.

Their words went right to my belly and gave me sad stomach.

"I didn't say things were better! I just said I like the beach!"

"You need to stop dwelling in the past," Alice said in her grandmother's grumpy voice.

"I'm not dwelling!" I yelled. "You don't know anything!"

I swam away from them, feeling hurt and confused. What was so wrong with preferring the beach to the pool? That wasn't being a snob. They were being mean.

My mom walked over to the edge of the pool and looked down at me. The pink nail polish she'd let me paint on her toes at the beginning of the summer had chipped, but she hadn't bothered to fix it.

"Everything OK?" she asked.

When our eyes met, I felt mine fill with tears.

"What's wrong?"

"I want to go home," I said.

"Home?" she asked, as if she wasn't sure what I meant.

"The apartment," I said. "Home."

I bet my mom was thinking of our other home. The one she loved and missed so much. I bet my mom wished we could go there now, instead of our crowded, hot apartment.

"But we just got here," my mom said.

I pulled myself out of the pool. "I'm leaving." I started toward our pile of towels heaped over the fence.

"Ivy!" my mom called after me. "You can't desert your friends!"

I turned to see Alice and Lucas pulling themselves out of the pool, looking confused and frustrated. My mom walked over to talk to them. Probably to apologize for my rude behavior. *She better not tell them to be nice to me!* I thought. She still treated me like such a baby sometimes.

I wiped my face with my towel and hid inside it as I cried into the scratchy old cotton. It smelled stale, like it hadn't been washed in a long time.

A hand touched my shoulder.

"Ivy," Alice said. "We're sorry. We didn't mean to hurt your feelings."

"You're only saying that because my mom told you to be nice." I pulled the towel from my face. "Do I really annoy you?"

"Everyone's annoying sometimes," Lucas said. "But we didn't mean to make you feel bad."

"I didn't like it better at my old house," I said. "I love it at Applewood Heights."

Alice and Lucas looked doubtful.

"Why would you like living in a stinky old apartment building more than a nice big house?" Lucas asked.

"It's not stinky!" I said. "And our house wasn't that

big. Or that nice. It was an old farmhouse that always needed fixing. And it was lonely there!"

"Why didn't you have friends over?" Alice asked.

"Because I didn't really have any. At least, not good ones, like you two. The kids I did know were all busy at summer camp, and my parents only had one car anyway, so it was hard to get together with friends when my dad had the car for work. I only had Rachel and Micah to play with. They were nice, but it's not the same as having friends your own age."

Alice and Lucas looked like they really did feel sorry for me.

"I didn't know you felt that way," Alice said.

"Me, either," Lucas agreed. "Sorry, Ivy."

I wanted to believe them, but I still felt hurt. I watched my mom waiting in the distance, pacing in the small, crowded space between the pool's edge and the fence.

"Let's forget about it," Alice said. "Please?"

"Yeah," Lucas agreed. "It was dumb. Anyway, let's go home. It's too crowded here."

We wrapped our towels around our necks as if they were fancy scarves and found my mom, who had struck up a conversation with another parent.

"You really want to leave already?" she asked.

I nodded, still feeling lousy inside.

My mom looked out at the crowded pool. "Maybe we can stop at the market and get some Popsicles," she said. "Would that cheer you three up?"

"Really?" I asked. We never did stuff like that anymore.

My mom ruffled my wet hair. "Really."

ᘡ Chapter Eleven ᘠ

At the market, we studied the frozen treat choices in the ice chest. There were all kinds of fancy ones, like the red, white, and blue treat in the shape of a rocket and an ice-cream sandwich made with chocolate chip cookies and chocolate-and-vanilla-swirl ice cream. But there was also a price sheet taped on the glass door, and those treats all cost about five times as much as a boring old Popsicle.

"Well, hello, friends," Brandi said, coming up to greet us. "Been to the pool?"

"What was your first clue?" Lucas asked, modeling his scarf.

"Hmm, the wet hair, I think," Brandi said. "Though I suppose you *could* have just taken a bath?"

"Not together!" Lucas said, blushing.

"Nice to see you, Brandi," my mom said.

Brandi smiled. "I hope you're getting yourself a treat, too, Mrs. Gartner."

My mom looked like she hadn't thought of that. "Good idea!"

I liked seeing my mom so friendly and happy. Usually she was too serious. I wished I had some money of my own. Then I would buy her the fancy cookie sandwich to *really* cheer her up.

Lucas reached for the ice-cream sandwich as if reading my mind.

"We can only get Popsicles," I told him.

He put the treat back and frowned. "I hate Popsicles," he said.

"No, you don't. You just want an ice-cream sandwich more," Alice said.

"Well, obviously. They're superior."

"Now who's being a snob?" I asked. I pulled out the open Popsicle box so we could each choose a flavor.

Alice took one out and pressed the white paper against the Popsicle to see what color it was. "Yuck. Orange." She put it back and chose another.

"Are there any blue ones?" Lucas asked.

I held the box out to him. The picture on the front showed red, orange, and purple.

He frowned again. "Fine. I'll take the orange."

I chose a purple and Alice's was red.

"Is red cherry or strawberry?" Lucas asked.

"It's just red," Alice said. "It doesn't really taste like either."

"I think orange is the only flavor that tastes like its name." Lucas started peeling the paper off his.

"We have to pay first!" I said. "You can't eat it before we pay." I turned to my mom. "Take one, Mom! Get purple like me!"

My mom pulled a Popsicle out of the box without even checking the color. "Let's pay for these before they melt," she said.

We followed her to the register and waited while she took out her wallet. The coin section was bulging with pennies that she carefully started counting out.

"Mom," I said. "Use the quarters. It's faster."

"But I want to use up my pennies," she said in a stern kind of way.

The guy behind the register rolled his eyes impatiently. I went from feeling annoyed with my mom for taking too long to wanting to help her. I didn't see why the guy was so impatient since there was no one in line behind us.

"Here. Pour some into my hand so I can help," I said. I handed my Popsicle to Alice and started counting.

When we finally handed over the exact amount, the cashier spread the coins on the counter and recounted them all. "You also have to pay sales tax," he said.

What a grouch.

My mom placed a few more coins neatly next to the others.

"You have a nice day," she said.

I wanted to tell him to try being more friendly, like Brandi, but my mom had gotten into a mood and I did not want to make things worse.

Outside, Lucas took a big bite of orange Popsicle.

"You're supposed to lick it!" Alice shouted.

"It's melting too fast! I don't want it to drip on my hand."

Alice and Lucas bickered a lot. So did Rachel and I, but we still loved each other, and that was how it seemed with Alice and Lucas. Even though Alice said I was her best friend, I wanted to feel close to her and Lucas that way. Different than best friends. Closer. Like family.

We walked back home slowly, licking our Popsicles and trying to catch the drips as they began to melt more quickly. At the building, we stopped and finished, licking our sticks for any last juice.

"Thanks for bringing us to the pool," I said to my mom before we went inside.

She gave me a little side hug. Her mood seemed to have picked up on our walk home.

"My pleasure," she said, squeezing me close.

"Yeah, and thanks for the Popsicle," Lucas said. He stuck out his orange tongue and touched the tip of his nose with it.

"Wow," my mom said. "I've never seen anyone do *that* before."

"Probably because it's gross," Alice said.

"You're just jealous because you can't do it!"

We all tried, but Lucas was right.

"We each have our own special talents," my mom said with a laugh.

I took Alice's and Lucas's hands and followed my mom inside.

"Home sweet home," I said, swinging our arms as we walked.

My mom turned back and smiled at us in her quiet way. I bet she was thinking about our old home and how much she missed it.

But for me, that home was already a long-ago

memory. I had a pillow that said "Home is where the heart is." When we had to move, Rachel got so mad she ripped it up. But I sewed it back together and brought it with us here. This *was* a sweet place. And it *was* home. How could I show the rest of my family that it was the best place ever? How could I convince them to want to stay?

I had to find a way.

Home sweet home, I thought instead of saying it out loud in front of my mom again. *It is. You'll see.*

❧ Chapter Twelve ❧

The following day was hot, hot, hot again. My mom got called to work from the temp agency, so I decided to find Donnalyn and see if she had any work for me. I loved being Donnalyn's helper. My favorite job was refurbishing bikes for kids who lived in the building. Last year, when we still lived at the farmhouse, I found a used bike for Rachel and fixed it up to surprise her for her birthday, and she loved it! So when I found out that Donnalyn collected parts to do the same for kids in the building, I jumped at the chance to help.

Alice, Lucas, and I didn't ride bikes much. Alice's bike was too small, but she refused to put her name on Donnalyn's list for a new one. She kept saying her bike was fine, but the few times we tried to ride together, her knees hit the handlebars when she pedaled, and it didn't look like much fun. Sometimes Alice could be so stubborn.

"Hello, Handy Girl!" Donnalyn called when I found her in her workshop on the first floor.

"Have any bikes for me to work on today?" I asked. "I'm bored."

"Got a few hopeless cases back there," Donnalyn said, waving to a corner of the room. "But I think we'll need to scavenge some parts to make them usable. You up for the challenge?"

"I'm always up for challenges," I said. I sauntered over to the corner where two bikes that had seen better days leaned sadly against the concrete wall.

"Hmmm. Where did you pick these up?"

"They were next to the dumpster out back, and I thought, If anyone can save these two, it'll be Ivy."

I felt my insides get all warm and gushy. I walked one of the bikes across the room closer to the light over Donnalyn's workbench so I could get a better look at it. The chain was off, and the rim on the front wheel was bent. Both tires were flat, and the brake pads were completely worn down. But the kickstand still worked!

I went and got the other bike, which wasn't in much better shape.

"I bet if I took the best parts from each bike, I could get one good one out of them!" I said.

"Sounds like a fun challenge."

Donnalyn kept a list of items people in the building needed, like bikes, strollers, cribs, and other household items. Then she'd visit the recycling center and thrift stores to see if she could find things she could fix up and give to tenants in need. I liked helping with all those things. But bikes were my specialty.

"Could you add one more thing to your list of needs?" I asked.

"Sure! What're you looking for?"

"It's not for me — it's for Mr. Stevens. He has trouble going places because his walker is so slow. I was thinking I could make him some kind of wheelchair, and we could push him."

"Hmm. I don't know if Mr. Stevens would want to be pushed around. He's pretty independent."

"He's on a waiting list to get a motorized scooter. I thought I could make him something helpful until he gets one."

"I think before you do that, you should ask him if he wants one, Ivy. He can be mobile with his walker. He may prefer that."

"But it could be fun! We could zoom him all over!"

Donnalyn took a slow breath, as if she was being careful of what to say next. "That might be fun for *you*, Ivy. And I know you mean well. But are you sure that's the kind of thing Mr. Stevens would enjoy?"

I imagined the chair I would convert, all decorated, with some foot holders to rig up so he could rest his legs. Maybe I could even find an old recliner like the one he had and put wheels on it. He'd be sure to love that. Who wouldn't? Why was Donnalyn being such a downer?

"Your heart is in the right place," Donnalyn said. "But it's important to ask if someone *wants* your help before you barge ahead. You might make him feel uncomfortable."

I nodded, but secretly I was sure Mr. Stevens would love to get a chair for a surprise. And I was going to make it happen!

"Well," Donnalyn said. "Time to make the rounds. I've got three light bulb changes and a torn window screen to repair. You want to tag along and help?"

"Yes!" I said.

"Great. Let's grab some tools and get to work."

I skipped over to the workbench to help gather supplies.

"You sure look happy all of a sudden," Donnalyn said as we put the tools we'd need together in two buckets.

"That's because I am!" I said. "I love fixing things!"

As we carried our buckets down the hall, I did my happy dance, making Donnalyn laugh. "I swear, Ivy, you sure can bring sunshine to a place," she said.

I grinned from ear to ear. "I do my best!" I said. I jumped in the air and clicked my heels, making the tools in my bucket clank around, then flashed my fingers wide, as if I was casting rays of sunlight down the hall with my hands. *Swoosh!* I could almost see them for real.

⚭ Chapter Thirteen ⚯

Every morning that week, I stopped by Donnalyn's workshop to work on my new bike project. I started with the easiest tasks: removing the parts I couldn't salvage and figuring out how to turn two broken bikes into one working one. I greased the chain Donnalyn found and put it on the better bike frame. I still needed to figure out how to repair one tire rim, but I had some ideas.

Whenever Lucas and Alice commented on how much time I'd been spending helping Donnalyn, I tried to explain how much I liked fixing things, but they didn't seem to understand. That was OK, though. I liked spending time with Donnalyn and learning how different tools worked. Maybe one day, I could be a repair person, too! That is, in addition to running my dream restaurant with Alice and Lucas.

On Saturday I grabbed my notebook and headed to Alice's. It was *Bake It to Make It!* day! I rapped on the door and waited, but no one answered. Odd.

"Hello!" I called at the peephole. "*Bake It to Make It!* starts in seven minutes!"

There was no sound on the other side of the door.

I knocked again. There had never been a time when Alice wasn't home. And we'd never missed an episode of *Bake It to Make It!* since we'd started watching together.

"Hello!" I called again. "Alice! Are you in there?"

Finally, I heard a shuffling noise inside, and Alice opened up.

"Where were you?" I asked. "We're going to be late!"

Alice's grandmother walked over to the door and stood behind Alice. They both had serious looks on their faces. Actually, sad and serious at the same time.

"What's going on?" I asked.

Mrs. Johnson took a deep breath. Her large chest heaved up and down.

"We got news about Stevie," Alice said.

Based on Alice's expression and the tone of her voice, it seemed like the news wasn't good.

"Oh," I said.

Mrs. Johnson put her hand on Alice's shoulder in a gentle way.

"She's not coming back. At least not for a long time." Alice's bottom lip began to tremble, as if she was letting the truth of the news settle inside herself.

"I'm sorry," I said.

"You go watch your show, dear," Mrs. Johnson said.

I had never heard Mrs. Johnson talk to Alice so tenderly. There was a kindness in her voice but also a sense of sorrow. It made the place in my chest where my heart was start to ache.

"I'll go get my notebook," Alice said.

I waited with Mrs. Johnson awkwardly. I wished I knew what to say, but I didn't want to ask her a personal question, which Rachel was always getting after me for doing. Had something happened to Stevie? Was she OK? Had she decided she didn't want to come back for Alice? I had so many questions! But I kept them to myself for once.

"Got it," Alice said, waving her notebook. She didn't seem very excited, though.

Mrs. Johnson nodded and patted Alice's shoulder. "Go on, it'll get your mind off of things," she said.

I tried to smile reassuringly. "Goodbye, Mrs. Johnson. We'll bake something special for you later!"

She nodded and shut the door.

Out in the hallway, I stopped.

"Well?" I asked.

"Well, what?"

"Why isn't Stevie coming back?"

Alice didn't smile or frown but shrugged a little bit. "I don't want to say."

"Why not? We're best friends." I knew I wasn't supposed to ask other people personal questions, but I thought it was OK to ask my best friend.

"It's just not something I want to talk about, OK?" Alice looked at the floor. It needed to be vacuumed, and a hole was starting to form where it was especially worn. Alice rubbed it with the tip of her sandal. I thought she was going to make the hole worse and she should stop, but I didn't say so. Instead, I watched Alice's cheerful ladybug flip-flops move in circles around the hole. They seemed out of place, the mood was so down.

I didn't understand why Alice wouldn't want to tell me what happened, but I decided not to push. "Well," I said, "on the bright side, this means you'll be staying here with me!" I smiled but noticed right away that

Alice's face had changed. Instead of looking sad, she looked angry.

"There is no bright side, Ivy!" she yelled. "That was a really insensitive thing to say! I want to be with my mom and now I can't! But you wouldn't know what that's like because your life is so perfect!"

"What?" I asked. My tummy lurched. That's not what I meant. And my life was not perfect! Did she really think that? The elevator opened and we stepped in.

"I meant I'm happy you get to stay here with me because you're my best friend!"

"It's not about you, Ivy! A best friend would know that. A best friend would be sad for me. A best friend would understand!"

"I *am* your best friend!"

"Not today!" Alice yelled.

Her words hurt so deeply, they made me feel sick. What could I say now? What could I do?

The door opened again, and she stomped out of the elevator and marched down the hall toward Lucas's place.

My heart pounded painfully. I didn't mean to hurt Alice's feelings! I chased after her down the hall.

Lucas swung open the door excitedly as soon as we

got close. He was wearing an apron with a spatula on the bib and the words GRILL OUT.

"Get it?" he asked. "Like 'chill out' only 'grill'!"

"Funny," Alice said, not laughing.

"Sheesh, what's up with you?"

"Nothing!" Alice said. "Let's just go in. The show probably already started."

"No," Lucas said. "Something's wrong. What?"

"I said, *nothing!*" Alice shouted.

I had never seen Alice get so mad.

Lucas stepped back. "Ohhhh-kay, then," he said as Alice pushed past.

Hot tears slipped down my cheeks. I quickly wiped them away.

"Did you two have a fight?" Lucas asked.

I nodded and cried harder. "I'm going home," I said.

"But you can't! We always watch together!"

"The show started!" Mr. Stevens called from the other room.

"You can make up after the show," Lucas said. "It'll be OK. All friends get in fights sometimes."

But this felt worse than a fight. I had really hurt Alice! I hoped Lucas was right, but in my heart, I was afraid I had ruined everything.

"Come on, Ivy. It'll be OK," Lucas said.

I nodded doubtfully and followed him in.

What I felt inside was worse than sad stomach. I was scared. And I was ashamed, too. I wished I could take my words back. If only I could have another chance to respond the way a best friend would. Was Alice right? Was I not a good best friend after all?

We took our seats on the floor in front of Mr. Stevens.

"You missed the theme song!" he said.

But I couldn't imagine wanting to sing along anyway. We all watched quietly. We didn't even take notes during the show. Nothing felt right. Nothing was right. And it was all my fault.

ℰ Chapter Fourteen ℘

After the show, instead of excitedly discussing how to make today's challenge like we usually did, we sat there, not talking.

Mr. Stevens seemed to notice something was wrong. "Well, I guess this week's ingredients would be too hard to find or too expensive," he said. "Show's getting too fancy, if you ask me."

Alice got up. "Thanks for letting us watch with you, Mr. Stevens," she said. Then she walked toward the door without even saying goodbye.

Lucas and I hopped up and followed. "Alice, wait for us! Let's go for a walk!" Lucas said.

"I can't. I'm going home." Alice started down the hall.

"Alice!" I called after her. "I'm sorry!"

"Come back!" Lucas said. "You two need to make up!"

But Alice didn't turn around.

I leaned against the wall in the hallway. "I ruined everything."

"What happened?"

I hesitated. Should I tell Lucas something Alice wanted private?

"Tell me!"

"Do you know about Alice's mom?" I asked.

"She left Alice here so her grandmother could look after her."

"Yes. And Alice has been waiting for her to come back."

Lucas nodded.

"Today Alice found out her mom isn't coming back for a long time. And I said something awful in trying to make her feel better."

"Why would you do that?" Lucas asked.

"I didn't mean to!"

"What did you say?"

I could hardly bring myself to tell him. I was so ashamed.

"Tell me!"

"I said, on the bright side, Alice gets to stay here with us."

Lucas rolled his eyes. "Oh, Ivy."

"I didn't mean to hurt her feelings! I was trying to help her see the bright side!"

"It's the bright side for you and me, maybe. But not for Alice. She misses her mom!"

"I know! I feel terrible. What can I do?" My stomach was feeling more and more rumbly and awful.

"Maybe you could write her a note to say how sorry you are."

"Yes! I could do that."

"But wait a little bit. She's probably too angry right now. And upset about her mom. Give her some time."

"OK." Tears began to slip down my cheeks again.

The doors to the elevator opened, and Donnalyn stepped out.

"Hey, you two! Ivy, you're just the person I was looking for!"

I sniffed and rubbed my wet cheeks with my arm.

"I need some small hands for a job. I've got a leaky pipe to tighten, but I can't fit my big mitts into the space I need to get to." She held up her hands to show us how big they were. Donnalyn was so strong, it seemed hard to believe there was anything she couldn't do.

"Do you want to help?" I asked Lucas.

"Nah. I'm gonna go keep my dad company." He turned and went back to his apartment.

I sniffed again.

"What's up with you?" Donnalyn asked, finally noticing I was upset.

"I said something mean by mistake, and now Alice is mad at me. And I think Lucas is disappointed in me."

"Uh-oh," Donnalyn said. "That doesn't sound good."

I thought about how nice it felt when she told me I brought sunshine to a place. Now it felt like I'd brought a giant rain cloud.

"I really hurt her feelings and I feel terrible."

Donnalyn adjusted her tool belt on her hips. "Well, then, you'll need to apologize."

"I tried! But she won't listen."

"Give it time," Donnalyn said. "You're all good friends. You'll work it out. C'mon. Let's go tackle this pipe and get your mind off your troubles for a while."

I nodded and followed Donnalyn back to the elevator. But inside, I felt as bad as ever. I couldn't imagine feeling better again. Not unless Alice could forgive me. But even then, I'd always feel terrible that I'd said something so insensitive.

What if Alice was right, and I didn't know how to be a best friend? What if I had ruined everything?

It was hard to believe that only yesterday, I'd been feeling so sunny and excited about the bike I was working on, and how much I loved living at Applewood Heights. My life had felt perfect! If only I could go back and not say what I had.

"Ivy," Donnalyn said, "I can tell you're letting what happened eat you up inside."

I rubbed my tummy. That was exactly what it felt like. As if a dark monster was inside my belly and eating up every last bit of happiness I had.

"I'm not a good friend," I said quietly.

"Oh, now. I know for a fact that is not true. All friends make mistakes sometimes. And you're not only a good friend to Alice and Lucas — you're a good friend to me! And all your neighbors here, too. Think of all the things you've helped me fix for others."

"I wish I could fix what I said to Alice."

Donnalyn nodded knowingly. "Where there's a will there's a way, Ivy. You'll figure it out."

I knew I had the will. I just wasn't sure about the way part.

ᕙ Chapter Fifteen ᕥ

Donnalyn knocked on Miss Beverly's door, and a loud voice inside called, "Who's there!"

"It's Donnalyn, Miss Beverly. And my trusty assistant."

There was a series of unlocking sounds, and the door creaked open. A small woman with big brown eyes blinked at us and waited, her hand still on the doorknob.

"I could oil those hinges so your door doesn't squeak," I said.

"What would I want a quiet door for?" Miss Beverly said. "Then I wouldn't know if someone was coming in uninvited!"

I hadn't thought of that.

"I'm Eunice Beverly," the woman said, stepping back to let us in. "And who do we have here?"

"This is my helper, Ivy," Donnalyn said. "I'm hoping she'll have better luck getting to that hard-to-reach pipe you have in the bathroom."

Miss Beverly nodded. "I've seen you running around with your friends. Pleased to meet you."

"Pleased to meet you, too!" I said. There was something about Miss Beverly that made me like her right away. She seemed to have what my dad would call a "no fuss, no muss" personality. Just my type!

I followed Donnalyn through the apartment, which was very neat and spare. The living room had a chair and a tiny tin-topped table next to it. There was a small TV hanging on the wall. There were no photos anywhere, but there was one bookcase overstuffed with books. I took a peek as we walked by. Holy smokes! They were *cookbooks*! I stopped and stared at their spines, reading the titles in wonder.

"Are these *all* cookbooks?" I asked.

Miss Beverly sized up the bookcase proudly. "That's right."

"But . . . why do you have so many?"

"Some people like reading romances or mysteries. *I* like reading about food!"

"Miss Beverly used to be a chef," Donnalyn said.

"Really?"

She nodded proudly.

I could hardly believe I was talking to a *real* chef! "What's your specialty?" I asked. "Mine's pancakes. I have a flair for raspberry with chocolate chips. My favorite show is *Bake It to Make It!* Do you watch it?"

Miss Beverly leaned closer to me to study my face. "I don't watch baking contests," she said. "They're no use to me. Why do you like that show?"

"It teaches me and my friends how to bake! We've learned all sorts of things, including how to improvise when we don't have the ingredients for a recipe."

"Improvise, huh? That's a big word for a small girl."

"I learned that word from *Bake It to Make It!*" I said. "Among other things." I wanted to point out that just because I was small didn't mean I couldn't know big words, but I was pretty sure that would sound rude.

Miss Beverly gave me a curious look and walked closer to the bookshelf. She pulled a big blue book down and petted the cover, as if it was an old friend. "You see this?" she said. "It's called *Larousse Gastronomique*. That's French. When I was a young cook learning the ropes, I studied it cover to cover."

"*La-roose Gas-troh-nom-eek?*" I repeated slowly.

"Close enough. If you really want to be a cook, you

should study this. You know who else used this book to learn to cook? Julia Child. Ever heard of her?"

I shook my head.

"She was a famous cook who had a *real* cooking show. No contests, just good cooking instruction. She swore by this book, and so do I. You can borrow it, if you'd like."

"But—it's so fancy!"

"Fancy schmancy," said Miss Beverly. "It will teach you all the basics and then some. Nothing fancy about that. Don't let the title fool you. Lots of explanations in there that'll give you a solid understanding of how to cook well."

I touched the silver embossed letters on the outside and said the words slowly. *"Larousse Gastronomique."* I opened the cover and read the first page. *"The Encyclopedia of Food, Wine and Cookery."*

"That's right."

"I can't drink wine!" I said.

"Well, you can cook with it, can't you?"

"I don't know if I'm allowed."

"Hmph. Course you are. The alcohol cooks away and it's harmless. Go on, take it."

"Are you sure?" I could hardly believe my luck.

"What do I need it for? I don't cook much anymore. Besides, I've got all that knowledge right up here." She tapped her temple. "You study that book and someday you will, too."

I held the book to my chest. Maybe . . . maybe Alice would talk to me again if she saw the book! Who could resist a whole book about cooking?

"Thank you!" I said. "I'll be really careful with it. I promise!"

Miss Beverly waved her hand. "The pages are covered with food stains already. Years of cooking in my old kitchen with that thing will do it."

"When I learn how to make something well enough, I'll bring you a serving."

Miss Beverly stared at me for a minute, looking surprised. "Well, that would be very nice!"

"Ivy!" Donnalyn yelled from the bathroom. "I need those small hands of yours!"

I followed her voice and found Donnalyn poking her fingers down the drain in the bathroom sink. "Open the cupboard below and see if you can reach this wrench in there and fit it around the coupling nut above the trap. You remember the diagram I showed you about plumbing under the sink, right?"

"Of course!" I set the big cookbook on the bathroom counter and got on my hands and knees. I could see where Donnalyn needed to reach and why she'd been having trouble.

"Did you find it?"

"Yup!" It was a tight squeeze, but I managed to fit the wrench around the nut. "Righty tighty or lefty loosey?" I asked.

"Tighty!"

I yanked the wrench and tightened the nut. "Got it!" I said.

"OK, now move back while I give it a try."

I crawled backward from inside the cupboard, and Donnalyn turned on the faucet. No leak!

"We did it!" I said.

Donnalyn turned the water on and off a few more times to make sure the water was flowing smoothly again and there were no other leaks. "Good as new!" she declared. "Nice work, partner!"

"I guess good things come in small packages," Miss Beverly said from the doorway.

I grinned and picked up the book.

"You enjoy that and read the entries carefully," Miss Beverly said. "Remember, it will teach you everything you need to know about cooking for the rest of your life. But the special part is, it will give you confidence to put your own twist on a recipe."

"Oh, I already do that!" I said.

Miss Beverly chuckled. "Well, then, you're off to a great start, dear."

I followed Donnalyn back out to the hallway and to the lobby.

"Do you have any other work for me today?" I asked.

Donnalyn grinned and crossed her arms at her chest. "I know you're hoping I say no so you can go devour that book."

I hugged it close to show her she was right.

"Go on," Donnalyn said. "You know where to find me if you need a taste tester."

I pressed the elevator up button and did my happy dance with the book, squeezing it tight as if it was magic. I couldn't wait to show it to Alice and Lucas.

"Please let them forgive me," I whispered to *Larousse*, whoever that was. "I promise I will never be a bad friend again!"

❧ Chapter Sixteen ❧

I ran down the hall to Alice's apartment clutching *Larousse Gastronomique*.

"Alice! Alice!" I yelled, banging on her door.

"Cut out that racket!" Mrs. Johnson called from inside.

I stood on my tiptoes to try to look through the peephole, but I was too short. Maybe if I stood on *Larousse* . . . but no. I could never do that!

I pressed my ear to the door and listened to Mrs. Johnson clomp toward me on the other side, then fell into the apartment when she swung open the door.

"Hi, Mrs. Johnson," I said. "I need to speak with Alice!"

The scowl Mrs. Johnson usually wore looked less scowlish and more droopy.

"Is everything OK?" I asked.

She shook her head and flicked her hand in the air like she was shooing a bug away.

"Alice doesn't want any visitors right now," she said matter-of-factly.

I felt my own body droop. *Visitors?* I didn't think of myself as a visitor. I was a best friend! At least, I had been. I stood in the doorway, not sure what to say.

"What's that you've got there?" Mrs. Johnson asked, gesturing to the thick book I was still holding to my chest.

"It's a special cookbook." I held it up so Mrs. Johnson could see better.

She squinted at the silver letters.

"It's French," I explained. "Miss Beverly from 104 let me borrow it. She said every good cook needs to study this book. I wanted to show it to Alice. As you know, Alice, Lucas, and I are going to be famous chefs one day and have our own restaurant."

Mrs. Johnson put her hands on her hips. She seemed about to say something but changed her mind.

"Well, that's nice. I'll tell Alice about the book."

"Could you tell her now? Maybe if she knew about the book, she would want to see me. I'm sure it could help cheer her up!"

Mrs. Johnson sighed. "I don't think so, dear. Alice needs some time alone for now. But I'm sure she'll want to see you soon."

She moved closer to the door so that I had to step backward, out into the hall.

"Do you really think so?" I wanted to feel hopeful, but it was awfully hard at this point.

Mrs. Johnson nodded. "Give her time," she said, and closed the door.

I decided to try Lucas next. I knew he would be as excited as I was about the book.

When he opened the door, a strong smell of garlic wafted into the hallway. Mr. Stevens was standing at the stove with his walker to keep his balance.

"Hi, Mr. Stevens! What are you making?"

"Meatballs!" he called over his shoulder. "Could sure use a hand!"

"What's that?" Lucas asked, gesturing toward *Larousse*.

"It's a special cookbook encyclopedia! Miss Beverly from 104 gave it to me. I tried to show Alice, but she's still not talking to me."

"Oh."

"Do you want to look at it? Or are you mad at me, too?"

Lucas shrugged. "Why should I be mad at you?"

"For what I said to Alice. And ruining our fun show-time."

"Hm" was all he said.

If he wasn't mad, he certainly didn't seem like his usual friendly self.

"Does that mean you'll look at it with me?"

"I can't. I'm helping my dad."

"Can I help, too?"

Lucas shrugged again. I really did not like that gesture of his. Just say yes or no! Care!

"Of course you can!" Mr. Stevens said. "We need to roll the last of these balls in some bread crumbs, but my leg is awfully tired. I'd be glad for the help."

"I was helping you," Lucas said.

"A third set of hands would be nice," Mr. Stevens said. "What are you so testy about?"

"Nothing," Lucas said.

I set *Larousse* on the kitchen table, then washed my hands at the sink and began to roll the meatballs in the bread crumbs and line them up on a cooking tray next to the ones Mr. Stevens and Lucas had already made. Mr. Stevens pulled up a chair by the kitchen table to rest.

"Too bad we didn't get to make the challenge today," Lucas said as he formed meatballs next to me.

So I was right. He *was* grouchy about the show. And it was my fault. Again!

"I'm sorry," I said.

"You say this is a cookbook?" Mr. Stevens asked, pulling the book closer to take a look.

"It's a cooking encyclopedia, to be more precise. Miss Beverly gave it to me. She said if Alice, Lucas, and I learn the terms and techniques described in this, we'll be real chefs!"

"That was awfully nice of her," Mr. Stevens said, flipping through the pages.

"Carly Lin and Dustin Kendal never mentioned that book," Lucas said.

"Well, they never mentioned Julia Child, either. But she was a famous TV chef, too. Miss Beverly said she was the best!"

Lucas made a face to show he wasn't impressed.

"Sure seems fancy." Mr. Stevens leaned forward to look more closely at a page. "I wonder what *Émincé* is."

This time, I was the one to shrug. But not in Lucas's grumpy way. "I dunno," I said. "But I'll learn how to make it. That's the point!"

"These ingredients sound expensive."

"We can be creative and do substitutes," I said. "Like when we don't have all the ingredients for our *Bake It to Make It!* challenges."

Mr. Stevens nodded, impressed. He rubbed his leg and made a face as if it hurt.

"Mr. Stevens, would you like me to make you a rolling chair to use until you can get your scooter?" I asked. "I've been thinking I could rig something up for you with wheels. We could push you all over, and you'd be able to get out and about more!"

Mr. Stevens stopped rubbing his leg and sat up straighter. "Oh, no. I don't need that." He made an awkward face. "I can get around fine enough myself."

"But it could be so much fun! I'm a pretty good inventor. I bet I could make something that would let you move much faster!"

"I don't need to move fast."

"But—"

"I said no, Ivy."

I'd never heard that tone from Mr. Stevens before. He didn't sound angry, like the time we'd all shared a toothbrush. More like . . . annoyed he'd had to say no twice.

Lucas glared at me. If looks could talk, he would have called me a terrible name.

Oh no. I'd done it again! Now I'd offended Mr. Stevens!

I covered my face with my hands. They smelled like meatballs, and I realized I'd gotten yucky meatball grease all over my cheeks. I quickly went to the sink and washed my hands, trying not to cry. I wiped my greasy cheeks with the hem of my T-shirt.

"Are you all right?" Mr. Stevens asked, starting to stand.

"Don't get up," I said. "I'm sorry. I meant well." Donnalyn's words came back to me. Why hadn't I listened to her? "I didn't mean to make you feel bad about the chair. It was just an idea I had."

Mr. Stevens looked confused. "That's all right, Ivy. I know."

"No, it isn't! I keep ruining things when all I want to do is fix them! I'm going home!"

Lucas didn't say anything. He didn't even *try* to make me feel better. And I didn't blame him.

"I'm really sorry, Mr. Stevens." I gave him a hug, grabbed my book, and left.

As I walked down the hallway, new tears began to slip down my cheeks. The elevator smelled like Ms. Medina again, but I didn't bother to try to take a deep breath in.

Alone in the elevator, I cried out loud. I really had ruined everything. Now Lucas was definitely mad at me, too.

I was starting not to love living here after all. What good was it if I didn't know how to be a true friend?

I didn't know how I messed up so badly. Alice should know I hadn't meant to hurt her feelings. Best friends were supposed to stick together, even when their words came out wrong sometimes. I said I was sorry! Alice was not being fair! If she'd just give me a chance to explain better, she would understand and everything would be fine again. Why was she being so stubborn?

The elevator stopped on my floor and made its familiar *DING!* before the doors slid open. In the short trip, I'd gone from feeling sad to feeling *angry*. I stomped down the hallway.

Rachel stepped out of the apartment with her backpack and noticed me storming toward her.

"Whoa, what's up with you?"

"Nothing!" I yelled.

She blocked me from going inside. "Ivy, what's wrong?"

"Alice and Lucas are mad at me! I said something insensitive to Alice, and even though I said I was sorry, she won't talk to me. And now Lucas is mad because our fight ruined *Bake It to Make It!* day, and then I hurt Mr. Stevens's feelings and made Lucas even more mad, and everything is TERRIBLE and I DON'T LIKE IT HERE ANYMORE!"

"Oh," Rachel said quietly. She put her hand on my shoulder. "I'm sorry. I'm sure you'll all make up. I have to go to work to do afternoon chores. Are you going to be OK?"

I brushed her hand off my shoulder. "It's Saturday! You don't even work on weekends!"

"The Townsends went away, and I'm working extra."

"Leave, then! Everyone else does! THIS IS THE WORST DAY EVER!"

Rachel looked like she wasn't sure what to do. "Mom and Dad went for a walk, but they should be back soon. Are you sure you're all right?"

I shoved past her. "I don't want to talk about it!" I ran to our room and slammed the door.

George was sleeping on Rachel's bed. He lifted his head when I stomped by. I swiped the curtain aside and fell facedown on my bed. *Larousse* tumbled to the floor.

I pulled my pillow over my head and sobbed.

ℰ Chapter Seventeen ℰ

George pressed his pointy little paws into my legs, then my back as he walked up my body. He poked his head under the pillow and purred into my neck. George might be the only one left who wasn't mad at or disappointed in me. I thought I'd better not say anything to him, or I might mess that up, too.

Rachel knocked on the door. "Ivy? Can I come in?"

I rolled over and let George settle on my chest.

She stepped to the foot of my bed and waited for permission to cross the invisible line that divided my side of the room from hers.

"I couldn't leave for work knowing you're feeling so bad."

"You can come in," I said.

She sat on my bed and leaned forward to scratch George behind his ear the way he liked. "Wanna tell me more about what happened?"

"I messed up."

"I figured that much. Want to tell me exactly how?" she asked.

"What good will it do? I always say the wrong thing. Everyone hates me."

"Oh, Ivy. That's not true."

"Yes, it is! I don't know how to be a friend. I don't know how to do anything right!"

Rachel put her hand on mine. "Just tell me what happened," she said.

"Alice told me her mom isn't coming back for her, and I told her to look on the bright side because it meant she could stay here with me and Lucas. And she was so angry at me, we didn't get to do our *Bake It to Make It!* challenge, so Lucas was mad at me for ruining that. And then I told Mr. Stevens I could make him a wheelchair so we could push him around, and I think I offended him because he can use his walker and doesn't really need to be pushed. I didn't mean to! I keep saying the wrong thing when what I mean to do is help people!"

Rachel frowned and twisted her mouth like she always did. I knew she was about to tell me what I said to Alice and Mr. Stevens was wrong. But I already knew that!

"I said I was sorry, but Alice is still mad. And Lucas gave me a horrible look when I made that comment to Mr. Stevens. I can tell he is really upset with me. How do I make things better?"

Rachel's shoulders rose and fell slowly as she thought some more.

"Sometimes words can be really painful," she said. "It takes more than an apology to make things OK. Sometimes it takes time."

"How *much* time? What if Alice never forgives me? What if Lucas thinks I'm a bad person? What if I don't know how to be a good friend? Why can't things stay the same? Why can't we all be best friends again and live here forever!"

"One thing at a time, Ivy. First, Alice doesn't want things to stay the same. She wants her mom back."

"Why can't she want both? Why can't she want her mom to come live here? Then Alice could have what she wants, but nothing else would change."

"I don't know," Rachel said.

My chest felt so heavy, and not because George was curled up on it. It was as if my heart had turned into a stone. "Why do things have to keep changing?"

Rachel reached for my hand and squeezed. "It's just how life is, I guess. I mean, if you think about it, there are only a few things in life that ever really stay the same. From the minute we're born, we change every day. And it's that way in relationships, too."

"But our relationship doesn't change."

"Sure it does. Sometimes you get mad at me, and sometimes you adore me." She nudged me and grinned. "But the thing that *does* stay the same is love."

"Even when you're mad at me?"

"Yes. I will always love you the same. And so will Mom and Dad and George."

"Well, I will always love Alice and Lucas, even if they don't love me back."

"Oh, Ivy. I'm sure they love you, deep down. This is one of those times in friendship where you have to figure things out. Micah and I have been in plenty of fights, but we always make up."

"Do you think I'll always be friends with Lucas and Alice?"

Rachel didn't answer right away. It made me feel nervous. Rachel was always thinking before she spoke. I sure wish I had done that today.

"I don't know if you will be. The best you can do is try."

George got off my chest and jumped to the floor. He sniffed my book and rubbed his face on the corner.

"What's that?" Rachel asked.

"A cooking encyclopedia that Miss Beverly from 104 gave to me. It's French! She told me if I read it cover to cover, I'll know everything I need to become a good cook."

Rachel picked it up off the floor and opened to a random page. *"Flangnarde,"* she read. "How do you pronounce that?"

"How should I know?"

"These instructions are pretty vague. Are you sure you'll be able to try all of these?"

"Of course not all. That would take a million years! But I can read about each recipe and technique!"

Rachel scanned the pages some more. "Ooh, this raspberry cream flan sounds good."

"What's a flan?"

Rachel flipped back to the beginning of the flan section. "Hmm. It sounds like what we would call a piecrust. I always thought it was custard, but maybe it's different in France. Like how they call soccer 'football' in England."

"They do?"

Rachel nodded. "It says here that it's a pastry that you put yummy fillings in. See?" She held out the book to show me the black-and-white photographs that illustrated how to prepare the crust. "Hmm. It looks like the filling is called 'flan' too. This book is confusing."

"I already know how to make piecrust!" I sat up to get a better look.

We spread the book across our legs and scoured the pages for more entries. I went to the kitchen for some sticky notes my mom used sometimes and began to mark pages with recipes that sounded fun to try and had ingredients that wouldn't be too hard to get.

"I bet if Alice and Lucas see how great this book is, they'll want to be friends again," I said.

"Ivy, you know that's not how friendship works."

This time I frowned. "I know."

Rachel looked me in the eye.

"*I know!*" I said again, to reassure her.

"Do you want me to cook with you? You could choose something while I'm off doing chores, and we can make it when I get back."

"Could Micah come over and cook with us, too?"

"Sure!"

"How come he hardly ever comes over anymore?"

Rachel shrugged. "He's been busy. He has a new girlfriend."

"Ooh! Who is it? Are you jealous?"

"It's no one you know. And no, I'm not jealous."

"Are *you* dating anyone?" I wiggled my eyebrows at her.

"Stop that! I'm not dating anyone right now. Not that it's any of your business."

"But I don't want you to be lonely!"

"I'm not lonely. I have plenty of friends besides Micah.".

"How come none of them come over?"

"I don't know!"

"You don't have to get upset."

"Then stop grilling me."

"Sorry." Was I messing up again? Saying the wrong thing? "I didn't mean to."

I closed the book and held it on my lap. "Is the reason you don't have friends over because you're embarrassed to show people where you live?"

"What? Why would you think that? No!" Rachel said.

"Well, you're always acting like you hate it here. So . . ."

"I don't hate it here. I just . . . miss how things used to be. There's nowhere to hang out here with friends. This room is too small, and Mom and Dad are always in the other spaces. It's not like home. Our old home, I mean."

"Yeah."

I realized that Rachel and I thought of our old house a lot differently. There, Rachel had Micah right down the street. But I didn't have anyone. Here, I had friends an elevator ride away, but Rachel didn't have anyone. I wished someone Rachel's age lived here. Then we could both have friends close by, and Rachel wouldn't want to leave, either.

"So," Rachel said. "Do you feel better now?"

I shrugged. "Not really. I'll only feel better when Alice and Lucas are my friends again."

"They'll come around. I'm sure of it."

"Have you ever heard of the saying about loving something and setting it free? It goes something like 'If you love something, set it free. If it comes back to you, it was meant to be.' I think that's how it goes, anyway."

"Yeah, that's a pretty famous saying. There are lots of versions of it, I think. But basically it's something like, 'If you love something, set it free. If it comes back to you, it's yours. If it doesn't, it was never meant to be.' Why?" Rachel said.

"I was thinking about Alice and Lucas. Not that I set them free. But . . . I was thinking about them coming back to me. I *know* we are meant to be friends forever. Like you and Micah."

"Huh. I don't think you're supposed to apply that saying to people, Ivy. I think it's about wild animals or something. Otherwise, it would be, 'If you love some-*one*.' Don't you think?"

"But that's what Alice's grandmother said about Stevie. She said she would come back if it was meant to be."

Rachel made her one-sided frown again. "That's like saying, 'Things happen for a reason.' But I don't think that's fair. Sometimes things just happen. It's not any-one's fault. No one deserved it. Life is hard sometimes. But hard things aren't meant to be. They're just . . . well, *hard*."

I nodded. Life was complicated.

"You know, Ivy, sometimes people don't want you to try to fix their problems. Sometimes all they need is to know you're there. And that you love them."

Rachel got up. "Eh. What do I know? I'm sorry you're going through a hard time. I hope things with Alice and Lucas work out."

She put her hand on my head like my mom used to do to her when she was feeling anxious. It felt as if she was trying to give me some of her calmness through her hand. It felt reassuring and warm, like saying "I love you" without the words.

"Thanks, Rach," I said.

I took a deep breath and let my chest rise up and fall back down. I decided right then that I would figure out how to make up with Alice and Lucas, no matter what. Promising myself that made me feel one hundred times better.

"Hey," Rachel said. "If Mom and Dad say it's OK, how would you feel about biking to work with me and giving old Rainbow a visit?"

I jumped off the bed and hugged Rachel harder than I ever had. "You mean it?"

"Let's ask them when they get back. But, yes! I mean it!"

୧ Chapter Eighteen ୨

After I made a million promises to stay to the side of the road and do everything Rachel said, my parents finally agreed I could bike to the other side of town and help with Rachel's summer job at the Townsends'.

When we turned onto our old road, a strange feeling crept through me. I wasn't coming home—I was visiting. Somehow, it made the road feel less familiar and less welcoming than when we lived here.

At the end of the Townsends' driveway, we stopped and looked across the street at our old house. The lawn was perfectly mowed and smooth-looking. When we lived there, the grass was always choppy and uneven where we let Rainbow graze on it. The house was freshly painted, too, and there were new flower beds planted in areas that used to be weedy and needed attention. Not only that, but the driveway, which had been cracked and always had grass and weeds growing in it, was newly paved.

"Wow," I said. "Imagine setting up our obstacle courses on that!"

Rachel, Micah, and I used to love making ramps and jumps for our bikes in the driveway.

"Right?" Rachel said. "They really fixed the place up."

I wondered if this was how my mom and dad imagined the house could look, if only they'd had enough money for flowers and paint and a new driveway.

"It doesn't really look like home anymore, though, does it?" I asked.

Rachel turned to me, then toward our old house again. "No," she said, as if suddenly realizing it herself. "Without us, it doesn't look like our home at all."

That seemed to be all we needed to say about that.

We parked our bikes in the Townsends' driveway, and I ran around back to find Rainbow.

He lifted his head at the sound of my voice and munched happily on the baby carrots I'd filled my pockets with. I pressed my face against his neck and breathed in his beautiful pony smell. Oh, how I'd missed him. I wrapped my arms around him and squeezed.

"You want a little ride?" Rachel asked.

"YES, PLEASE!"

She hitched a lead on him and gave me a leg up. While we walked around the grounds, Rachel reintroduced me to all the animals.

First the goats: Agatha and Christie. Then the sheep: Ewe and Me.

Each time, Rainbow stuck his nose over the fence to say hello and sniff, and the animals would come up to us and sniff back. Rainbow flicked his tail, and it tickled my bare legs.

"You know, it seems you've gotten a lot taller since the last time you rode him," Rachel said. "Your feet dangle almost to the bottom of his belly!"

I wiggled my legs. "He seems happy, doesn't he?"

Rachel nodded. "He found a really good home."

"And he still gets to see you almost every day!"

"Yup."

Rachel led us to an overgrown fenced-in area where a pig named Lucy used to live. She wasn't very nice to Rachel, but we'd tried to make friends with her. The Townsends had raised her for meat, though, not as a pet. And now she was gone.

"I'm glad they didn't get another pig to raise," Rachel said. "Mr. Townsend told me he was going to take down the fencing and plant some grass here, but he hasn't gotten around to it."

I slid off Rainbow and brushed his hair from my legs. "Thank you for the ride, buddy!" I gave him another hug.

"You want to feed him?" Rachel asked.

"Of course!"

I helped Rachel bring him to the barn and filled his grain bucket. Then I watched him eat happily while Rachel fed the other two horses, Ben and Gil. I braided Rainbow's mane the way we used to and brushed his dusty coat.

"Do you wish we still lived across the street?" I asked Rachel through the slats in the stall.

"I miss living near Micah, and having Rainbow at our house, and reading to you in the backyard. We have a lot of good memories."

"Maybe we could try to make good memories at Applewood Heights. Then you'd like it there better." I thought about all my good memories there so far, before I made Alice and Lucas mad at me.

"It's not so bad there," Rachel said. "At least the apartment doesn't get as cold in the winter. Remember how we used to freeze at the old place?"

"Yes! It was so cold, the bedroom windows got frost inside them."

"And you tried to write 'Save me!' in the frost with

131

your fingernail, but I made you cross it out because I was afraid people would see it and think you were being held prisoner!"

I giggled. "Yeah, you were no fun."

"Hey!"

"Kidding!"

We walked back out to the barnyard, and I tagged along while Rachel fed all the other animals.

"I can't stop thinking about Alice and Stevie," I said as we spread chicken feed for the hens.

"Alice must be awfully disappointed that her mom isn't coming for her."

"Yes," I said. I realized guiltily that I hadn't given enough thought to that—I'd been so caught up in wanting Alice to forgive me. Poor Alice! I *was* a terrible friend. I thought of the way Alice waited at the door for Stevie every day, hoping she'd come back. It must be the saddest, loneliest feeling in the world! I wished there was something I could do to help. But I think Rachel was right. Sometimes you can't fix other people's problems. But I *could* let Alice know I was there for her. And that I loved her.

We gave the animals their water and sat on a grassy mound to watch Rainbow and the other horses.

"He seems really happy," I said again.

"Yup. Sometimes what feels like the worst change can turn out to be the best."

"Sometimes," I said.

Rachel put her arm around me and pulled me close.

Some changes really do seem like they were meant to be. And some are a lot more complicated.

"I still don't like that saying," I said.

"What saying?"

"The 'meant to be' one."

"Well, yeah. I bet we could find a flaw in all kinds of sayings people use."

"Like . . . you snooze, you lose?"

Rachel closed her eyes and made a snoring sound. I tickled her.

"Don't rely on sayings to tell you how to live your life," Rachel said. "Just be a good, kind person. Be a good friend."

I rested my head on Rachel's shoulder. "I'll try," I promised.

Rachel took a breath before she replied, probably to tell me I had to do more than try, but I stopped her before she could.

"I mean, I will," I said. "I will."

❧ Chapter Nineteen ❧

The next morning, I prepared to visit Alice and tell her how sorry I was. I picked up *Larousse* and hurried down the hall, holding the heavy book in both hands. I knew Rachel was right, that a book can't win a friend back. But I still felt hopeful that if I apologized *and* showed Alice the book, she would want to be friends again. Besides, I was positive the book would help cheer her up!

I arrived at Alice's feeling hopeful, but instead of Alice, Mrs. Johnson came to the door. My heart sank in my chest like a deflated balloon.

"Good morning, Mrs. Johnson," I said. "I came to see Alice."

"Well, I figured you weren't here to see me," Mrs. Johnson said.

I grinned. "I like to see you, too!"

Mrs. Johnson smiled a little, but it quickly faded. "Alice is in her room and says she still doesn't want to have visitors."

My balloon heart shriveled. "But—"

"I'm sorry, Ivy. Alice got some more hard news about her mother this morning, and she isn't up for friend time."

"Hard news about not coming back?" I asked.

Mrs. Johnson nodded. "Not for quite some time."

"How come? Is she all right?"

Mrs. Johnson sniffed and blinked, as if she was trying not to cry. It's what my dad did when we watched sad movies together. I knew what that felt like and wanted to tell her to go ahead and let it all out. That's what my mom always said to me, and it usually helped.

"It's private," Mrs. Johnson said.

"Oh." I remembered Rachel's advice not to ask personal questions about Alice's mom. All I knew was that she had a problem with drugs, which is how Alice put it. I hoped something bad hadn't happened, but something must have if Stevie wasn't coming back. What more bad news could there be? I hoped she hadn't gotten hurt.

"I'm sorry, Mrs. Johnson," I said. I reached for her hand and squeezed it.

Mrs. Johnson looked surprised at my touch and squeezed back. Her eyes were red and saggy, the way my mom's got when she didn't sleep well. I stepped forward and hugged her around the middle, pressing *Larousse* between us.

Mrs. Johnson patted me on the shoulder in a gentle way, like she had to Alice earlier.

I always thought Mrs. Johnson was gruff, but maybe she was trying to be strong. Now it seemed like all her strong parts were gone.

"Will you tell Alice I came by?" I asked, stepping away from our hug. "I wanted to try to show her my book again, and to tell her I'm sorry for saying something insensitive. I really didn't mean it. I wish she knew that."

"I will," Mrs. Johnson said. "You run along now and come back another time."

"OK." I hesitated in the doorway. Maybe I could make Alice feel better if I could just talk to her. But Mrs. Johnson was already trying to shut the door.

I decided to find Donnalyn and work on the bike for a while. I still needed to test the chain and a bunch of other things that would keep me busy and maybe take my mind off missing Alice.

"How goes the bike project?" Donnalyn asked when she came over to check my progress. "Fixing it up good as new?"

"Still needs a lot of work," I said, touching the bike frame. "But I can do it."

"Of course you can," Donnalyn said.

"Do you ever wish you could fix more than *things*?" I asked.

Donnalyn looked surprised. "Well, sure," she said. "Don't we all?"

"What would you fix?"

"Hmm. The state of the world, for one. Feels awful broken sometimes. How about you?"

"I'd make it so Alice and her mom could be together," I said. "Even if it meant Alice would have to move away. I don't like it when Alice is so unhappy. Or Mrs. Johnson, either."

Donnalyn nodded. "People are a lot more complicated than bikes. And relationships are sometimes the hardest things of all to fix."

I nodded but hoped that wasn't the case with me and Alice.

I fit the chain on the wheel and moved the pedal with my hand to make sure it worked. The wheel spun, but it looked like the rim might be warped.

"Alice is still mad at me," I said. "I told her I was sorry, but it didn't help. She's so mad, she won't even talk to me."

"Ah, that's rough. But I'm sure she'll come around."

"That's what Rachel said. But I'm not so sure. If she would only talk with me, I think I could make it right. And I think she could really use a friend right now."

"Lucas is her friend, too, no?"

"Yes," I said. "He is. But I am, too! At least, I want to be. But I ruined everything." I spun the wheel faster. "And I think Lucas is mad at me, too, because I offered to make a wheelchair for his dad, and I hurt his feelings."

"Oh, Ivy. We talked about that."

"I know! But I really thought he would like it!" I spun the wheel even faster.

"Easy there," Donnalyn said. "Don't get your hand caught in the spokes. That would hurt!"

I grabbed the wheel to make it stop. It was going so fast, it burned the inside of my hand, but I didn't care. I closed my eyes and took a long, deep breath in, then let it out. Rachel taught me to do that when I feel myself winding up and getting upset.

"I just want things to be like before! I don't like

change. Rachel said things are *always* changing. But I wish that wasn't true. I hate change!"

"Nothing stays the same for long," Donnalyn said. "That's one thing you can rely on."

"Ugh! You sound like Rachel. Some things *should* stay the same! Don't you think?"

Donnalyn turned her back to me while she inspected something at her workbench. It looked like a light switch box. I watched her back rise and fall, as if she was taking deep breaths, too. Was Donnalyn mad at me now as well? I wasn't sure I could take one more person being disappointed in me.

"I'm a go-with-the-flow kind of person," Donnalyn finally said. "I've learned to try to roll with the punches. Especially when they're out of my control."

"Too many sayings!" I yelled before I could stop myself.

Donnalyn chuckled. "Aw, Ivy. You sure are in a mood today. I hope you and Alice mend fences soon. And Lucas, too. Oops, I mean, I hope you make up soon. Good friends always do."

I began to spin the wheel again. The rim was definitely warped and would need to be replaced. It seemed like everything in my life was broken. I found a wrench and took the wheel off the bike frame and set to work taking off the tire, which I could still salvage. But a replacement wheel wouldn't be easy to find. Maybe my dad could take me to the recycling center. They sometimes had old bikes that people were getting rid of there.

"You know what we need?" Donnalyn said. "Some good tunes."

She turned on the radio at her workbench and found a station playing oldies songs. She began to bop her head to the beat. "That's what I'm talking about!" she said, swinging her hips.

But I couldn't get into it and decided to give up for the day and go home. It was the first time I hadn't had fun working in Donnalyn's workshop, and I was feeling more miserable by the minute.

At home, I sat on the couch with George and tried to read *Larousse*. I got the sticky notes from the kitchen to mark which recipes I thought would be fun to try with Alice and Lucas, but making cooking plans without their input was no fun. *Nothing* seemed right without them. I was beginning to wonder if I loved Applewood Heights after all.

ᏟᏟ Chapter Twenty ᏅᏅ

The following Saturday, it was the season finale of *Bake It to Make It!* I'd taken everyone's advice and waited a few days before trying to talk to Alice again, and I'd decided to do the same with Lucas. But I was lonely! I worked on the bike every morning, then helped Donnalyn with chores. I kept telling myself to wait for Saturday, when Lucas and Alice were sure to want to watch the big show together.

"It's almost time for your show!" my dad pointed out at breakfast. He was eating peach pancakes I'd made and declared them his favorite yet.

I knew it was time, but I was afraid to go to Alice's apartment. What if she still wouldn't talk to me?

But I had to try.

I gathered my cooking notebook and *Larousse*, took a deep breath, and left.

"Is Alice here?" I asked when Mrs. Johnson opened the door. I already felt dread. If Alice didn't come to the door, it probably meant she still didn't want to see me.

"She is," Mrs. Johnson said, "but . . ."

"Please let me speak with her, Mrs. Johnson. I need to!"

Mrs. Johnson sighed. "She just needs some time, Ivy. I'm sorry, dear."

I felt my bottom lip quiver. I did not want to cry in front of Mrs. Johnson!

"Will you tell her I was here? Please?"

"Of course. You run along. It's your show day, isn't it? I'll try to get Alice to watch here. Maybe it will cheer her up, and she'll want to bake with you later."

"OK," I said. But I didn't feel very hopeful.

"Where's Alice?" Lucas asked when he opened his door.

"She's still upset with me," I said. "Are you still mad, too?"

"No," Lucas said. "I was only annoyed. Sometimes you are a little too pushy and don't think before you speak."

"I know," I said. "I'm sorry. I shouldn't have brought up the chair to your dad."

"It's OK," Lucas said. "I know you wanted to help. But, Ivy, next time, I hope you'll listen to me."

"I will," I said. I felt so relieved, I wanted to hug him.

"And don't bring it up again," Lucas said. "Not even to say sorry to him. OK? Just drop it."

"But I *am* sorry. I want him to know—"

"Ivy!" Lucas interrupted, clearly starting to get mad all over again.

"OK!" I said. "I won't say anything."

We went into the living room, and I tried my best to be cheerful toward Mr. Stevens. I got comfortable in my usual place on the floor next to Lucas, my notebook at the ready. But it felt different without Alice.

"I hope today's challenge is a tough one," Lucas said.

"It's the season finale! I'm sure it'll be good."

"Right!" Lucas fidgeted excitedly as the theme song came on and the announcer introduced the judges.

"It's tiiiiiiime for *Bake It to Make It!* with your judges . . ." There was a long pause.

"Sorry, folks," the announcer said. "I wanted to make sure I read that correctly. Let's try this again. It's tiiiiiiime for *Bake It to Make It!* with your judges, Carly Castle and Dustin King-dal!"

The two strode out dressed as a king and queen, with silly crowns on their heads.

"Castle!" I yelled. "We're going to make some sort of castle!"

"With cake?" Lucas asked.

"Yes!" we both shouted together.

"Shhhh!" Mr. Stevens said. "I can't hear!"

Lucas and I high-fived and giggled.

The judges introduced the contestants and waited for the applause to die down before they revealed the secret ingredients in the Pot-Pourri. Under the cloth was a child's plastic sandcastle bucket and shovel. Inside the bucket was cocoa powder, flour, eggs, and sugar.

"Hmmm," Mr. Stevens said. "Looks like they have to make a sandcastle cake."

"You can't bake a cake in a plastic bucket," Lucas said. "The plastic would melt in the oven."

"I bet it's for show," I said. "To get us in the beach mood."

The timer went off and the contestants began mixing the Pot-Pourri ingredients, plus others from the staples cupboard they were allowed to use to make their concoctions, like salt and baking powder. They were told they could use any cake form they wanted.

One contestant made two sheet cakes and connected them to make a long rectangle that was meant to look like a beach towel.

"Way too simple," Lucas said. "Besides, the judges clearly want a castle."

Another contestant tried to create a "drip" castle, making a Bundt cake that he said he'd drip frosting on after to create one of those muddy castles kids make at the beach.

"Clever!" Lucas said. "I think we should try something like that."

"Yes!" I agreed. "We could make light-brown icing to look like sand!"

"Maybe mocha flavored!" Lucas said.

"I like the way you think!" I wrote down our ideas in my notebook.

In the end, the beach towel looked like a big lumpy cake that was way too thick to resemble a towel.

"I sure wouldn't want to lie down on that!" Carly Lin told the contestant.

The Bundt cake didn't rise properly in the oven and ended up looking like a deflated beach ball, so the baker decided to decorate it bright red.

"Don't throw this thing around," Dustin Kendal said, sticking his fork into the cake.

The third contestant had made a cake that he cut

and decorated to look like a crab, but the cake hadn't cooled enough when the contestant frosted it, so the icing had melted off the cake.

"My goodness," Carly said. "Looks like this poor crab was out in the sun too long. I didn't know crabs could melt!"

Dustin shook his head and adjusted his crown. "These sure are disappointing results, friends. Not a castle in sight."

The contestants all hung their heads.

"We can do better!" I yelled at the screen.

"We'll make the best drip castle ever!" Lucas agreed.

I quickly made a sketch in my notebook and showed Lucas.

"Yes!" he said. "What do you think, Dad?"

Mr. Stevens leaned forward in his chair. "Looks good to me!"

"We have to get Alice," Lucas said. "We can't do it without her!"

I jumped up, feeling excited. Then I remembered.

"What?" Lucas asked, noticing my frown.

"She's still not seeing visitors."

Lucas threw up his hands in an exasperated way. "We have to fix this!"

"I've tried!"

"Fix what?" Mr. Stevens asked.

"No time to explain. Come on, Ivy. We are going to Alice's right now."

My heart lifted a little bit. It felt like this heavy thing I'd been carrying inside ever since Alice stopped talking to me became a bit easier to hold.

"Best friends stick together," Lucas said in his matter-of-fact way. "Best friends figure things out."

I threw my arms around Lucas and held tight. I was so grateful to hear that he thought of me as a best friend, just like Alice had. And maybe could again.

Lucas squirmed. "Ack! Not so tight!"

I stepped back and grinned at him. "Let's go!"

ᘓ Chapter Twenty-One ᘖ

"I sure hope she will talk to us," I said on our way to Alice's.

"She'll come around," Lucas said. "She always does."

"You've been in a fight before?"

"Of course. Loads of times."

"I don't remember you two ever fighting."

"Well, sometimes it's not obvious. Sometimes she just gets quiet for a while. Like now. Try not to take it personally, Ivy. Alice is probably really worried about her mom, and sometimes she doesn't know how to handle her emotions. Sometimes she takes it out on her friends."

"Like that time at the pool when she said I was annoying?" I asked.

"Yeah. Like that."

"It must be hard to be worried all the time."

Lucas nodded.

I thought about how it would feel not knowing when I'd see my mom again. It made me want to cry. I wished I could make it better for Alice, but I knew I couldn't. All I could do was try hard to be a better friend. And I knew I could!

Lucas knocked on the door and waited, but no one answered. We tried three more times, but still there was silence on the other side of the door.

Finally, we gave up.

"We'll try another time," Lucas said.

We decided to sit outside at the picnic table placed in the shade of the apartment building to scour *Larousse* for the perfect cake choice, but all the cakes required too many ingredients and didn't seem like they would make good castle cakes. We had to figure out how to make a cone-shaped cake so it would look like a real sandcastle.

"Maybe we could make a sheet cake, and then cut lots of different-sized circles to stack on top of each other, like a tower," Lucas suggested.

I got out my notebook and drew a diagram. We'd need to make a lot of sheet cakes to have enough layers to get the cake tall enough to look like a castle.

"This reminds me of the skyscraper cakes they tried to make on *Bake It to Make It!*" Lucas said, studying my drawing. "Remember how they all tipped over?"

"That was because the cakes were too light, and they collapsed when they settled. Maybe we could make something more dense, like fruitcake."

Lucas made a face. "Fresh fruit would be delicious, but candied fruit is gross. My grandma sends us a fruitcake at Christmas, and it's disgusting."

"I guess you're right. Besides, do we want to stick to the challenge or add our own ingredients? Candied fruit would definitely be cheating. I wish Alice was here. She likes to break the rules for a good cause."

"I say we find whatever type of cake we think would stand the best chance of being dense enough to build a tower with *and* that we can get the ingredients for," Lucas said.

"*And* that tastes good," I added.

"Of course."

I picked at the splintered wood on the surface of the picnic table. It occurred to me I should really come out here and sand it smooth so no one gets a splinter.

Lucas continued to flip through the pages of *Larousse*. It seemed like neither of us knew what to say anymore.

"Do you think Alice is meant to be with her mom instead of her grandma?" I asked. "I mean, eventually?"

"It seems like that's what she wants. She's wanted her mom to come back for a long time."

I nodded. "She's always standing on that stool, looking."

"I hope she comes back, if that's what would make Alice happy."

"Me too," I said. "Oh, I wish we could help Alice! I hate not being able to make her feel better."

"Sometimes friends need some space," Lucas said. "That's what my dad says."

"I wish I never told her to look on the bright side. It's a terrible thing to say when someone is feeling bad. What I meant—what I should have said—is that I love her, and I was glad we'd all be able to stay together."

"I think she knows that, deep down."

"I hope so, because I really do. I love both of you."

"Don't get so mushy," Lucas said.

"Why not?"

"I don't know. It's embarrassing!"

"I just want you to know how I feel."

"I get it," Lucas said. "Let's change the subject."

"I wish my family wanted to stay here as much as I do," I said.

"I meant change the subject to something that isn't sad!"

"Oh. Sorry. I can't help it. I can't stop worrying about moving."

"It's not really up to you whether your family moves or not, Ivy. It's up to your parents."

"I know that. But if I could convince them—"

"Ivy. This isn't a place for all families to stay forever."

I sighed. I knew that was true. I just hadn't wanted to accept it.

"It doesn't change how I feel," I said. "I want to stay here with you and Alice. Forever!"

"I know."

"If I have to move, I'll come visit you every Saturday so we can still watch *Bake It to Make It!* and cook together."

"You know everyone who leaves says they'll come back to visit, but they never do, right?"

"You mean like Becka?"

"Yeah."

"She hasn't been gone too long. I bet she'll be in touch. She said she would have a sleepover party. Remember?"

"Don't hold your breath," Lucas said.

"Well, I'm not everyone. And the three of us are

meant to be friends. Whether we all keep living here or not. Friends forever!"

I reached over and held out my hand and stuck out my pinkie. "Swear it!"

Lucas hooked his pinkie with mine. We nodded quietly, as if to settle it once and for all.

"Friends forever," I said.

Lucas tightened his pinkie around mine, and we shook on it. "Promise."

I thought about what it would be like to move away from this place and away from my friends. And wondered how soon it would be. What if we had to move before Alice forgave me? We *had* to make up before then.

I thought again about Donnalyn saying, "Where there's a will there's a way." I would find one. I had to.

❧ Chapter Twenty-Two ❧

On Monday I went back to Donnalyn's workshop to work on the bike. Donnalyn had found another junk bike for me to take parts from, and my "new" one was nearly ready!

I used a rag to clean the dried-up dirt off the pedals. I wanted the bike to look brand-new for the lucky owner. I imagined who it would go to. Someone around my size would be best, since it was perfect for my height.

Then I realized: *Alice!* I knew she insisted her old bike wasn't too small, but maybe if she at least tried this one and saw how much better it was, she'd take it. Then the three of us could ride bikes together. If the cookbook couldn't cheer her up, maybe this could!

I ran over to Donnalyn, who was busy trying to fix the electrical wire on an oscillating fan.

"Donnalyn! Can I see the waiting list for the apartment kids who want a bike?"

She stood up straight and stretched her back. "I know it's around here somewhere. You ready to send this bike on its way?"

"Yes! And I know just the person to give it to, if there isn't anyone else my size on the list."

Donnalyn gave me a look. It reminded me of the warning she gave when I got excited about my wheelchair idea for Mr. Stevens.

I knew it was wrong to give the bike to Alice if her name wasn't on the list and someone else's was. But with Becka moving away, there weren't any other kids my size besides her . . .

"Let me go look," Donnalyn said. She came back holding a clipboard with a rumpled piece of paper attached to it. There were names on a long list, but most had been crossed off, thanks to me!

Donnalyn began to read a few names but noted those kids were little and not ready for the bike I'd fixed. "There's also Mr. Jackson. He's been wanting to ride a bike instead of taking the bus to work . . ." She eyed the bike. "But that's way too small for him."

"I know someone who needs a bike whose name is not on that list," I said.

"Now, Ivy. If a person didn't ask for something, it's not your place to—"

"I know!" I interrupted. "But this person . . . I know she needs one. Because she outgrew hers. And I bet it would really cheer her up!"

"You wouldn't be talking about Alice, would you?"

"Yes," I said. "And before you think I want to give it to her because I want her to be my friend again, that's not it. I just think a nice new bike could make her feel better."

"If Alice wanted a new bike, her name would be on the list," Donnalyn said.

"She has a bike, but it's way too small. She just won't admit it!"

Donnalyn gave me her uncertain look again, and now I was sure she was thinking about the time I hurt Mr. Stevens's feelings. Right away, doubt slowly grew in my heart. I'd tried to fix things before, only to make them worse.

"Let me think about it," Donnalyn said. "But since there's no one on the list, I don't see why you shouldn't offer it to Alice. If you're sure it's a good idea, that is."

"I think it is," I said. "Or I hope it is."

"Come back when you're sure," she said, almost

sternly. Some people really held grudges. But I knew why she said it that way. I hadn't listened last time.

I nodded.

"All right, then. You're a good friend, Ivy. I know you'll figure out what the right thing is." She said it almost like a warning.

"I will," I said. "Promise."

All that week, while Lucas and I worked on plans for our sandcastle drip cake, I secretly daydreamed about surprising Alice with the bike. The more I thought about it, the more certain I was that Alice would be glad to have it. Who wouldn't? But first, we had to get Alice to talk to us again.

We continued to scour the pages of *Larousse* and studied various techniques for baking cake and using cake forms. Of all the *Bake It to Make It!* challenges, this one was definitely the hardest. It would have been the most fun, too. But it wasn't the same without Alice.

Lucas and I agreed that we'd wait a bit before we tried to reach out to Alice again. But it was hard not having her be a part of our planning. It didn't feel right. It was like being on a bike stuck in one gear when you wanted to go faster, *faster*, FASTER.

Finally, after days of trying to figure out what kind of cake to make for our sandcastle without any progress, we decided to try to see Alice again. But when Mrs. Johnson opened the door, our hearts sank.

Mrs. Johnson stood in the doorway, frowning. I wanted to hug her again, but I wasn't sure if that was OK. It seemed as though ever since she and Alice learned that Stevie wasn't coming back, something big had changed inside both of them.

"Mrs. Johnson," I said. "Did something bad happen to Alice's mom? Is that why Alice is so sad?" I knew it was private, but I couldn't help asking. I waited for Lucas to nudge me or tell me I was rude, but he didn't.

Mrs. Johnson's bottom lip quivered. I had never seen her show so much emotion before.

"I'm sorry, Mrs. Johnson. I didn't mean to upset you. I'm just so worried about Alice."

Mrs. Johnson patted my shoulder. "That's all right, dear. I know you mean well." She looked at the two of us before saying more. Her brown eyes glistened, and she blinked away the tears forming in the corners.

"Stevie . . ." She paused. "Well, Stevie got herself in some trouble."

"Trouble?" Lucas asked.

"It's none of their business!" Alice rushed up behind her grandmother. "Why can't you leave me alone?" she yelled.

Alice did not look like Alice. Her hair was all clumpy as if she hadn't washed or brushed it in days. Her face looked hollow, and the area around her eyes was red and swollen.

"Alice!" I stepped forward to hug my friend.

Alice jumped back. Mrs. Johnson tried to put an arm around her, but Alice moved out of her reach, too.

"Why do you keep coming here? I told you I don't want any visitors!"

"We're not visitors," Lucas said. "We're your friends!"

"Same thing!"

"Alice!" Mrs. Johnson said. "Don't be rude. Lucas and Ivy are here because they care about you."

I didn't know what to say. Alice looked like a stranger. I'd seen Alice get angry but never like this. My stomach immediately started to hurt.

"We're sorry," I said quietly.

"We only wanted to check in and make sure you're OK," Lucas added. "We watched the season finale of *Bake It to Make It!* and thought you might like to cook the final challenge with us."

Alice glared at us. "That's all you care about! That dumb show! There's more to life than baking!"

"Hush, Alice," Mrs. Johnson said.

"No! I will not hush!" Alice yelled.

"We're so sorry," I said again. "We didn't mean to upset you. We thought we might be able to cheer you up."

"Well, you can't cheer me up! OK?" Alice shouted. "No one can!"

I hung my head. I wished Lucas would say more, but he seemed at a loss for words, for once.

"Why don't you two come in," Mrs. Johnson said. "We don't need everyone on the floor hearing us."

We stepped all the way into the small kitchen, and Mrs. Johnson closed the apartment door. There were three chairs at the table, but no one sat. I wondered if the third chair was meant for Stevie. Maybe Mrs. Johnson believed she was coming back just as much as Alice did, even if she hadn't said so.

"Come into the living room," Mrs. Johnson said. "Alice, you too. It's time you three talked about all of this."

"I don't want to," Alice said.

"I know that. Ivy, Lucas, you sit on the couch."

We did as we were told. Alice stood with her arms

crossed at her chest. She was wearing her pajamas and by the look of it hadn't changed them in a long time. The bottoms were all stretched out at the knees. The top was too small so that the sleeves didn't even come close to her wrists. I thought it was strange that she was wearing what seemed like winter pajamas in the middle of summer.

"Now," Mrs. Johnson said, her voice much softer than usual. "As you know, Alice had some hard news recently about her mother. I didn't think it was my place to tell you. And it doesn't seem like she wants to talk about it. But, Alice, you can't change what's happened. Now it's time to move forward. And your friends here have shown up over and over to let you know they care about you."

Alice didn't move from her stance across from the couch. She stared at her toes.

No one said anything.

The tears I'd kept from spilling slowly slipped down my cheeks. I quickly wiped them away with the back of my hand.

"I don't see why *you're* crying," Alice said to me. "You have a mom *and* a dad *and* a sister. What do *you* have to cry about?" She gave me a hateful glare.

"Why are you so mad at me?" I asked. "I would

never purposely hurt your feelings. I just want to be your friend again."

"You didn't even answer my question," Alice said.

I thought carefully before I spoke. "I'm crying because I'm sad for you. And I miss you. I don't know what happened, but I want to help you feel better."

"So do I," Lucas said.

"You see?" Mrs. Johnson said. "Ivy and Lucas are good friends."

Alice didn't answer.

"Please, Alice," I said. But I wasn't even sure what I was asking for.

"What do you know about anything?" Alice said. "You don't know what it's like to worry."

"I do," said Lucas.

"Well, I wasn't talking to you."

"I do know what it's like," I said. "When we lost our house, we didn't know where we would live—"

"Oh, poor you. Most people never have a house to lose in the first place. I'm supposed to feel sorry for you?"

"Alice Louise Johnson, what has gotten into you? I know you are hurting, but that is no way to treat your friend. I did not raise you to behave like this!"

"You didn't raise me! Stevie did!"

Mrs. Johnson shook her head. "Not in the last two years, she didn't. And no granddaughter of mine treats good friends like this. I can guarantee Stevie wouldn't like it, either."

Now it was Alice's bottom lip that began to quiver. She looked so tired and now overwhelmed with sadness on top of it.

"It's not fair!" she finally cried out. "I waited and waited. You said Stevie would come back if it was meant to be. And it *is* meant to be. I know it is!"

"It still can be," Mrs. Johnson said gently. "It still can, my girl. You'll just have to wait a bit longer is all."

Alice shook her head. "I can't wait any longer. I'm tired of waiting. I'm tired of hoping and then being let down."

Mrs. Johnson put her arms around Alice, and Alice sobbed into her grandmother's chest. She rubbed Alice's back as Alice heaved her sadness against her.

I wished I could go and hug them both, but Lucas and I stayed on the couch and waited until Alice was all cried out.

I felt I'd said the wrong things all over again. Alice was right. Worrying about where to live wasn't the same thing as worrying about a person you loved. It *had* felt scary at the time. At least, in lots of ways. But I had never been afraid of losing my mom or dad or Rachel. We only lost a home. Not a person.

When Alice quieted, I stood.

"Alice," I said carefully. "I'm sorry. You're right. I don't know what this is like for you. And I'm sorry I said things to make you feel worse. I didn't mean to. I promise."

Alice sniffed.

"What happened to Stevie?" Lucas asked.

Alice wiped her face and lifted her eyes to meet her grandmother's.

"That's something Alice can share if she wants to. In her own time." Mrs. Johnson rubbed Alice's back again. "Why don't you get changed out of these silly old pajamas and—"

"They're not silly! They're the last thing Stevie got for me."

Mrs. Johnson's mouth dropped. She seemed horrified that she hadn't realized. "I'm sorry, sweetheart. I didn't know."

Alice looked down at her too-small pajamas. No one seemed to know what to say in that moment. It was all too much. I thought about her too-small bike and wondered, *Is that why she didn't want a new one? Because Stevie had gotten it for her?* Maybe Donnalyn was right.

If Alice wasn't on the list, there was a reason. I felt sad, thinking I wouldn't be able to give the bike to Alice after all. But then Alice lifted up her arms to see how short the sleeves of her pajamas were. And then she lifted one leg to show how the bottoms came up to her shin. She smiled the tiniest smile.

"It's all right," she said. "Maybe they are a little silly."

"Silly or not, why don't you put on some play clothes and go spend time with your friends. It'll do you good to get out of this apartment."

I wanted to shout, *Yes! Come on!* but I waited for Alice to decide.

Alice looked at us shyly. "I'll be right back," she said.

❧ Chapter Twenty-Three ❧

When Alice returned, she was wearing cut-off shorts and my favorite tie-dyed T-shirt.

"So, what do you want to do?" she asked.

A happy warmth spread all through me. I don't think I've ever smiled as much as I did at that moment. "I'll go get *Larousse* and meet you at the picnic table so we can start making plans! Lucas, you fill Alice in on what we've figured out so far. And bring your notebooks!"

When I met them at the table, Alice already seemed a bit less hollow-looking. I couldn't stop grinning—I was so happy to see her. But I was also nervous. I didn't want to say the wrong thing again and ruin everything.

"Hi," I said shyly, as if we had to learn how to be friends all over again. "Did Lucas tell you about the sandcastle cake?"

"Yes! And about how you don't know how to make it."

"Ha!" It was good to hear Alice had her signature sass back. "Well, that is true. Do you have any ideas?"

"Not really."

"Maybe we should go visit Miss Beverly," I suggested. "I bet she'll have some good advice. I have a feeling she knows how to cook everything!"

We gathered our cooking notebooks and went back inside.

We all knocked on Miss Beverly's door at the same time.

"Well, look who's here," Miss Beverly said when she opened her creaky door. "The next Julia Child and her sidekicks."

"Which one of us is the next Julia Child?" Lucas asked.

"Well, I know I'm not her sidekick," I said.

"Me, either!" Lucas said.

"This is Lucas and Alice," I told Miss Beverly, who held out her tiny wrinkled hand.

Alice shook it. "Not a sidekick, either," she said.

Miss Beverly laughed. "You can all be the next Julia Child. Better yet, be the next great chefs. You can be partners."

"That's the plan!" I said. "Someday we're going to run our own restaurant together." I turned to Alice and Lucas. "Right?"

"Right!" they both said.

"So, what brings you here?" Miss Beverly asked.

"We want to make a special cake, and we came for advice," I told her.

"What kind of cake?"

"One that looks like a sandcastle," Lucas said. "But not the fancy kind you make with buckets that are already shaped like a castle. The messy kind."

"My sister, Rachel, and I call them drip castles," I explained. "You drip wet sand on top of a mound, and it looks like a mud palace."

"Hmm. I know what you mean, but how would you do it?"

"The drip part can be frosting," Lucas said. "It will have to be the right consistency. Not too firm and not too wet."

"It's the cake part we aren't sure about," Alice added. "We need to make a sandcastle-shaped mound somehow that is strong enough not to sink or tip."

I beamed at the sound of Alice's voice. I couldn't help it! It felt so good to have her back. I wanted to hug her and never let go!

"We thought maybe we could cut a sheet cake in different-sized circles and pile one layer on top of another," I said. "But we'd need a really dense cake that wouldn't start to tip over with all the weight, like Alice said."

"Hmm." Miss Beverly turned and walked into her tiny kitchen. We followed close behind.

"Bend down and open that cupboard for me, will you?" She motioned to the cupboard next to the stove.

Lucas opened it, and I peered in.

"Not sure I kept the molds, but they're worth looking for. Ivy, pull out all the pans there and see if there's a set of circular molds way in the back. I haven't used them in ages, but I might have kept them."

Alice and I began moving pans from the cupboard and handing them to Lucas, who placed them on the small table in the middle of the kitchen. There were springform pans and Bundt pans and brownie tins and a tart mold. We knew what they all were from watching so many episodes of *Bake It to Make It!*

Miss Beverly continued to watch over my shoulder. "No . . ." she'd say. "Not that one. No . . . not that one, either."

"I've never seen so many different pans all in one place," I said. "You must have baked every kind of dessert there is!"

169

Miss Beverly grunted in a proud way. "And how."

Way in the back corner was a set of circular tins nestled inside each other. They didn't look like something you could make a cake with, but I pulled them out anyway, because I wanted to know what they were for.

"That's it!" Miss Beverly said. "I think these are perfect."

"These?" I held them up in disbelief.

"Yup! Those are molds for making *kransekake*."

"*Kranse*-what?" Lucas asked.

"It's a Norwegian cake. I haven't made one in, oh, thirty years, I bet. I can't believe I hung on to those old things."

Alice inspected the cake forms. "I don't see how you make a cake with these."

"You see, each of these circles makes a ring. The batter is thick and cooks more like a cookie than a cake. When they've baked, you take them out of the form and stack them, biggest one on the bottom, and then all the way up to this tiny one here. Traditionally, it's a sweet almond flavor, and you use white icing dripped down the sides in a pretty pattern. But you could drip your icing, in this case, to make it look like a sandcastle!"

Miss Beverly seemed as excited as the rest of us.

"I think that would work!" I said. "But the cake would have to be chocolate, so it will be brown like sand."

"We're supposed to use cocoa, according to the challenge," Lucas said.

"It's an almond cake," said Miss Beverly. "But I don't see how adding a little cocoa would hurt."

"Chocolate makes everything better," Lucas said. "Do you think *Larousse* has a recipe for *kranse*—what's it called again?"

"I have a recipe I'll lend you," Miss Beverly said, pushing past us to get to the bookcase in her living room.

"I hope the ingredients aren't too hard to find," Alice said.

"Where there's a will there's a way!" said Miss Beverly. "Let's see what it calls for before starting to fuss with worry."

"Where there's a will there's a way," I repeated. Donnalyn had said so, too. And she'd been right! It would be the same with the cake. I knew it. I looked at Alice and smiled for the hundredth time. I thought about the bike I wanted to surprise her with and hoped I could pull it off. I couldn't wait to put some finishing touches on it, now that we were friends again. But of course, I'd need to check with Mrs. Johnson to make sure she thought it was a good idea.

Still, I felt a happy warmth run all through me. My mouth wasn't just smiling—my whole body was smiling! If someone told me today might be the happiest day ever, I never would have believed it. But it was!

❦ Chapter Twenty-Four ❧

"I can't remember ever having this many people in my kitchen," said Mrs. Johnson on our big baking day. She was wearing an outfit I'd never seen before. Usually she wore her housecoat and slippers all day. But today she was wearing a red sweater, a dark purple skirt, and brown shoes with shiny buckles.

It was fun to see her looking so happy and to have her welcome us in, rather than telling us to go play somewhere else.

We spread out our ingredients on the small table in the middle of the room. The only thing we'd added that wasn't included in the original challenge was almonds, but we'd decided to make an exception.

"My goodness, you three are certainly organized," Miss Beverly said. "And did you blanch and grind the almonds yourselves?"

"Yes!" I said proudly. "Getting almonds was the hardest part because no one in the building had any to contribute, and we had to beg my big sister, Rachel, to buy them for us. We have to give her the first bite of the cake as payment."

"Blanching the almonds was the best part!" Lucas said.

We took turns explaining how we'd followed the recipe Miss Beverly had given us to boil the almonds, then cool them and squeeze them out of their skins.

"We shot a few across the room at first," Lucas said. "But we got the hang of it fast."

Miss Beverly laughed.

"Grinding them up was even more fun!" Alice said. "We didn't have a food processor or grinder, but Ivy borrowed a hammer from Donnalyn."

"A hammer?"

"Yup!" I said. "We wrapped the nuts in a dishcloth and took turns smashing 'em into dust!" I swung my hand as if I had a hammer in it.

Mrs. Johnson chuckled.

"Let's get baking!" Lucas said.

I placed the recipe on the table, and we all leaned over to see what needed doing first.

"You know how to separate an egg, I presume?" Miss Beverly asked.

Lucas nodded, but when he picked up an egg, his fingers trembled.

"Go on, you can do it!" I said.

"Or I can," Alice said. "I can even crack an egg with one hand!"

"Show-off," Mrs. Johnson said. But she had a proud look on her face.

"There are three eggs. We can each do one," I said.

One by one, we separated the yolks from the whites in two bowls, then measured the rest of the ingredients, including the added cocoa.

Miss Beverly hovered over us as we mixed and stirred, nodding and giving her opinion as we went.

"Look at them go," said Mrs. Johnson. "It's thanks to that show they watch. They've learned to bake all kinds of treats."

"What a lucky woman you are, to have your granddaughter live with you."

The room got quiet.

I knew what Miss Beverly meant. Alice's grandmother *was* lucky. And Lucas and I were lucky, too, to have Alice living here. Because we loved her. But I knew now that Alice didn't feel the same way. Not if it meant she wasn't with her mom. Miss Beverly meant well, but I was certain her words hurt.

Words were powerful.

I thought about all the silly sayings people used to explain things again. It was hard to say the right words or to know which words could hurt, even if you didn't mean them to. I'd sure learned that.

"Time to put the dough in the forms!" Lucas said, changing the subject.

"Yes!" I said, glad to help him.

"This is the fun part," Miss Beverly said. "Making dough worms!"

We divided the dough into sections and followed her instructions to roll it out, making long worms the thickness of the forms. Then we carefully fit the worms into the forms. We placed all the forms in the oven and sat around the table to wait.

I shared a chair with Alice and Lucas since there were only three. Our bums barely fit, but we didn't care!

Since we had our notebooks, we described our restaurant plans to Miss Beverly. And she shared stories about being a baker at different restaurants, and what it was like. Mrs. Johnson told us about her job as a waitress, at diners and then in fancier restaurants, and how, when Stevie was born, she brought her to work, and the staff would pass the baby around to help take care of her. Eventually, she had to leave Stevie at home with her own mother because she couldn't afford a babysitter.

"Restaurants are in my blood, I guess," Alice said. She smiled a little, and it made me smile, too. I wondered how often Mrs. Johnson shared stories about Stevie.

Mrs. Johnson reached over and touched Alice's hand. "They sure are," she said.

"Tell us more stories!" Lucas said.

As the two women talked, they began making "Oh, I know" faces, especially when they told us about the difficult customers they'd had to contend with. It was fun seeing them get to know each other. Maybe they would become friends, just like Lucas, Alice, and I had!

When the timer went off, we set the forms out around the counter on various folded dishcloths to cool, and the stories continued.

"Why didn't you tell off some of those mean customers?" Lucas asked.

"Oh, we couldn't do that, or we might lose our jobs. The customer is always right, eh, Miss Beverly?" Mrs. Johnson said.

"Well, I won't put up with them at my restaurant," Lucas said.

"You could lose business," Mrs. Johnson pointed out.

"Why would we want to do business with rude customers?" I asked. "Rachel says, you shouldn't live your life by some old sayings, and I think 'The customer is always right' is one of them!"

The women looked at each other and smirked.

"This next generation isn't putting up with nonsense," Miss Beverly said.

"Indeed," Mrs. Johnson agreed.

We checked the cakes by touching them gently. "Still a tiny bit warm, but I think we could start preparing the icing now," Alice said.

We had brought the double-boiler contraption I'd concocted after a special chocolate-themed episode of *Bake It to Make It!* where Dustin Kendal gave a big lecture on the proper way to melt chocolate without burning it. I'd used Donnalyn's workshop tools to cut metal coat hangers with her special snips, then bent them to make a stand. I carefully placed it inside one big pot and poured water into the pot. Then I set a smaller pot on top of the wire stand so it rested above the water.

"My goodness, is that your own invention?" Miss Beverly asked. "Impressive!"

My insides felt mushy with pride. Alice nudged

my hip in her old familiar way, as if to say, *Way to go!* I beamed.

We melted the chocolate Brandi had given us at a special price because it had gone past its sell-by date but was still fine. Then we added butter until it was all melted and smooth.

"Add the confectioners' sugar slowly," Lucas said. "We have to keep testing the consistency until it's right for making drips like mud."

I lifted the wooden spoon we'd been stirring with and let the icing drip off, then Alice added more sugar and stirred until it thickened and the drips held their shape.

"Looks like mud to me!" said Miss Beverly.

When the cake was completely cool, we turned the circles out onto the table. Starting with the biggest one, we began to make a tower, spreading icing between the circles like cement to hold them together. Slowly, they formed a cone-shaped structure.

"It really does look like a sandcastle!" Alice said.

Lucas tilted his head one way, then the other, as he studied the structure. "Or like a giant poop emoji," he said.

"Lucas!" I yelled. But I had to admit, he was right. No matter—soon we'd cover it up with icing.

"What did he say?" asked Miss Beverly.

"Time for the drips!" Alice said, changing the subject.

I pulled out a used freezer bag I'd brought. I had triple-washed and dried it and kept it in my box of cooking supplies for just such an occasion.

"This will be our pastry bag for the icing," I said.

Lucas used the wooden spoon to scoop the remaining icing into our makeshift pastry bag. I took a pair of scissors from my box and carefully snipped the tip off one corner.

"Clever trick!" Miss Beverly said. "I've had to do that myself from time to time. It's not the most reliable, since the hole can begin to rip and make the piping too thick, but it'll do in a pinch."

"Sometimes you have to make do with what you have," I said, quoting a contestant from *Bake It to Make It!*

"That you do," said Miss Beverly.

"You go first with the icing," I said to Alice.

She bit her bottom lip and held the bag over the base of the cake tower. Slowly, the icing oozed out as if she was letting mud slip through her fingers to create the drip-castle look.

"Marvelous!" Mrs. Johnson said.

I'd never heard her say that word before, and it made me grin.

Miss Beverly leaned in to inspect the drips. "They're holding their shape."

"Now you take a turn." Alice handed the bag to Lucas. "My hands are tired from squeezing!"

Lucas began to make his way up the cake, letting the drips slowly ooze down the sides. Right before he got to the top, he handed the bag to me.

I squeezed out the last of the icing, letting it collect in drips like I remembered doing at the beach when I was little and Rachel taught me how to make a muddy castle.

When it was done, we all stood back to admire our creation.

"Truly a work of art," said Miss Beverly. "I'm impressed!"

"*Now* it looks like a sandcastle," Lucas said. "I wish we had a camera."

"Rachel's phone has one!" I said. "And we promised her the first taste for getting us the almonds." I ran to the door and turned. "No one move! I'll be right back!"

ᠻ Chapter Twenty-Five ᠵ

In the elevator, I did my happy dance. I couldn't wait to show Rachel how perfect our cake turned out. But mostly I was relieved to have Alice back. We really *were* meant to be!

When I got to our apartment, I skipped over to my parents and Rachel, who were sitting at the kitchen table looking at some papers that had photos of houses on them. They looked like the listings my dad made of the houses he was trying to sell.

"You sure look happy," Rachel said.

"Our sandcastle cake is done and it's perfect! Will you come take a picture with your phone? And also, you can have the first bite, like we promised!"

"Sure!" she said, starting to get up.

"What are you all looking at?" I asked.

My mom shuffled the papers around. "Oh, we were just looking at some new listings your dad made this week."

"There's a little farmhouse," Rachel said. "But it's too expensive."

"Too expensive for what?" I asked.

"Us," said Rachel.

My mom put the photos back in the folder.

"It's not a listing for us," my dad said, shooting Rachel a glare. "I showed it to your mom because it's the kind of place we'd like to move to. Someday."

"But not now," I said. "Not for a really long time. Right?"

"Well, not *too* long," Rachel said. "I love you, but I need my own room." She gave me a pretend punch in the arm, but I did not think it was funny.

"That's awfully privileged-sounding of you," I said. Lucas taught me what "privileged" meant, and I knew I was right.

Rachel rolled her eyes. "We can't stay here forever. You know that."

"But things finally just got better! Alice is my friend again! And I still have to give her my big surprise! We can't move! We can't!"

My heart started pounding in my chest, and I had that familiar, horrible swarm-of-bees-trapped-inside kind of feeling.

My mom pulled me close for a hug.

"Don't worry, honey. We aren't going anywhere for a while. We were only looking for fun. Daydreaming is all. We promise we will tell you when we're ready to start looking seriously. You'll have plenty of time to prepare."

My cheeks grew warm with anger. "Why would you daydream about leaving when you know how much I love it here? I don't want to move! My best friends are here! And Mrs. Johnson and Miss Beverly! And Donnalyn!"

"Ivy, you know our situation here is temporary," my dad said softly. "You've always known that."

I didn't want to cry, but the tears came anyway. I felt the way I did when we found out we had to move the last time, and I worried about Rainbow, and where he would go. No, that wasn't true. This time, I felt even worse. Rainbow found a better home. But I knew things wouldn't change for the people I left here. And it wouldn't be better for me, either! I would never find friends like Alice and Lucas again. Never!

"None of you care what I want! We could stay here longer, but you don't want to, even though I do!"

"Ivy," my dad said. "Of course we care."

"We're sorry you're upset," my mom added. "We love you and don't want you to be sad or worried."

"Well, I *am* sad and I *am* worried!" I yelled. I picked up the folder of listings they'd all been looking at and threw it across the table. The papers scattered, some of them faceup, some facedown. Photos of pretty houses and empty rooms with big windows and clean floors stared back at us.

"Ivy!" my mother said. "That's no way to behave!"

I glared at Rachel. "The whole reason I came up here was to share the cake with you. But you can forget it!"

"You're acting like a baby," Rachel said.

It was as if the angry bees in my chest exploded out of me. I picked up one of the papers strewn across the table that had a photo of a pretty farmhouse on it and ripped it in two. Then I stomped out the door and slammed it with all my strength.

No one followed after me.

I stood in the hallway and sobbed, waiting for someone to come out and say they were sorry and promise we wouldn't have to move. Not ever again.

But no one came, and after a while, all my tears dried up.

I slid down the wall and sat on the floor. The carpet smelled funny, like a wet dog, but I didn't care.

Change, change, change. Why did everything have to keep changing?

I was supposed to convince my family how special it was here, and I failed. Now they were all daydreaming about moving to another old farmhouse. Probably in a neighborhood without any kids my age. Probably far from Applewood Heights. So far, it would be hard to visit my friends.

The door to the apartment opened.

"Ivy," my mom said gently. "Would you come back in here, please?"

"I don't want to talk about moving!" I yelled.

"We don't have to. But we need to discuss what happened."

She reached out her hand, and I took it. She pulled me up and wrapped her arms around me. I rubbed my cheek against her soft T-shirt.

"We love you very much. And we know you love living here. We're sorry if talk of moving someday upset you."

"It did," I said. "It does."

She hugged me tighter. "I'm sorry," she said again. "I'm sorry for this emotional roller coaster we've put you on."

I had never thought about it like that. About how emotional it was, living this way. Not knowing what was around the corner. I thought about all the emotions I'd had since we had to leave our old home and come here. I started out being sad and scared and nervous. But then I'd been happy and glad and grateful. And excited! And proud! And then I'd been sad and scared and nervous again. Up and down. Fast and slow. Fun and scary. It *was* like a roller coaster.

I squeezed my arms tight around my mom and held on, as if we were both on the roller coaster right now and she could keep me safe.

"I don't like emotional roller coasters," I said into her shirt.

"I know, honey. I know. It's not fun at all."

I thought about the emotions she and my dad and Rachel also must have had during this time. It hadn't been much fun for any of them. I was the only lucky one. I'd made friends and loved it here. But they were all still worried about money. Rachel missed Micah and didn't get to hang out with her friends like she used to. My mom and dad missed their garden and fixing up the old house of their dreams.

I realized I'd been pretty selfish, thinking about what I wanted all the time and not what they wanted. Why hadn't I thought more about their feelings? It was just like with Alice when I'd been so insensitive. I was so focused on the news that we'd stay together longer, I hadn't thought about what it must be like to miss her mom so much.

I stepped away from my mom and took her hands. "I'm sorry, Mom. I'm sorry I acted so selfish and threw those pictures."

"It's all right, honey."

I knew she meant it, but I also knew it wasn't really true.

❦ Chapter Twenty-Six ❧

After apologizing to my family and picking up the papers I'd made a mess of, I went back to Alice's without Rachel or her phone. Having Rachel there would remind me of what had happened, and I didn't want to think about it.

When I got there, the door was open a crack, and I could hear them all laughing inside. Lucas was telling everyone about the pool and his theory about the water. "It doesn't really turn purple when someone pees in the water," he said. "That's a scare tactic. So, you know there must be a *lot* of pee in there with all those little kids in the pool. Since the water doesn't turn purple, there's no way to really know!"

"Mm-hmm," Miss Beverly said. "I am sure you are right."

"In that case, I'd rather take a cold shower or bath to cool off," said Mrs. Johnson.

"We should get a kiddie pool!" Alice said. "We could set it up in the living room and pretend it's a posh indoor pool and sit in it and watch *Bake It to Make It!*"

Everyone laughed at the thought. They went on like that for a bit, while I sulked outside. I had expected them to be quiet, waiting for me to return. Or at least to be wondering where I was, since I'd been gone so long. But no. They were having fun without me. They didn't even miss me!

I wanted to go in and tell them it was mean to talk about the pool like that. For a lot of kids, it was the only fun place they could go to in the summer when it got so hot. And I would point out to Lucas that now *he* was acting privileged.

But instead, I only listened. Is this what it would be like when I moved away? Would they all be fine without me? Would they miss me at all? They certainly didn't seem to need me now.

I felt more lonely than I had when Alice was mad at me. I sniffed, trying not to cry again.

"Hey! What are you doing out there?" Lucas said, coming toward the door. "Were you spying on us?"

I shook my head.

"Where's Rachel? Did you get her phone? Wait." He looked at my face more closely. "Have you been crying? What's going on?"

I shrugged.

"Rachel's not coming, so we can eat the cake without her," I said. "We can save her a piece for later."

"Did something happen to her?"

"No. And I don't want to talk about it."

"All right." He bumped my hip the way Alice always did, as a way to say, *We're over it. Let's go have some fun.*

But was I over it? Would things ever stay the same for once?

"There you are!" Mrs. Johnson said. "We missed you!"

Alice looked up and smiled at me. "Come on, Ivy! We've been waiting and waiting for you to get back!" She rushed over and took my hand and led me to the table.

Sometimes, when people are unexpectedly nice to me, it makes me get a little teary. As my eyes began to well up, I blinked away my tears and forced a smile.

"Let's dig in!" Lucas said.

I swallowed all my angry, sad, scared roller-coaster feelings down and bumped Lucas playfully. "Let's eat!" I said.

But I was only pretending to be excited. It was too

hard to be truly happy when I knew that soon, the unsure feelings I had about the future would twist and turn inside my tummy again, making me wish I knew what was meant to be and what wasn't. And why. *Why, why, why.*

❦ Chapter Twenty-Seven ❧

I suppose the sandcastle cake tasted pretty good, but I didn't really notice. I couldn't stop thinking about the house listings my parents were daydreaming about. Would there ever be a time when my parents wouldn't have to worry about money? Or wonder where we'd live next? I'd been so focused on my own worries, I hadn't thought about what they'd been going through. And I felt terrible.

After we had our share of the cake, we delivered the *kransekake* to our regular donors to try. I let Lucas and Alice do all the talking.

"What's up with you?" Lucas asked when we got to his apartment. "You sure seem mopey."

"Yeah," Alice said. "You've been strange ever since you came back without Rachel's phone."

I shrugged. "Remember when I said I didn't want to talk about it?"

"Yes," Lucas said.

Alice nodded.

"Well, I still don't."

I held the remaining *kransekake* while Lucas opened the door.

Mr. Stevens was asleep in his chair.

"Did you want to bring some of this to your family?" Lucas whispered.

I shrugged again.

"Ugh, would you please tell us what's going on?" Alice looked both concerned and scared. "We're best friends, and best friends can tell each other anything."

"That's right," Lucas said. "We're all three best friends. Through thick and thin."

I made myself smile at them. "I'm glad we're best friends."

"We are, too," Lucas said. "Now tell us what you're hiding."

"I'm not hiding anything—I just don't want to talk about it."

"That's kind of the same thing," Alice said.

"It makes me feel blue. And I think it will make you

feel blue, too. Today was such a fun, special day, mostly. I don't want to ruin it."

"I know what it's like to get hard news," Alice said. "I spent a lot of time not wanting to talk about it. But I feel better now. And I bet you will, too."

I could feel my sadness reaching up the back of my throat and into my eye sockets. If they said one more nice thing to me, I knew I would start to cry again.

"Is it about Rachel?" Lucas asked.

"Kind of. It's about my family."

"Is someone sick?"

"No."

"Ivy, tell us what's up. You'll feel better. We can handle it." Alice touched my arm in a kind way, the way I'd seen her grandmother touch her recently. Having Alice try to comfort me like that made me feel special.

Lucas set the *kransekake* on the counter and sat on the kitchen floor, out of sight of Mr. Stevens in the next room.

Alice and I sat down next to him. I picked at a piece of linoleum that was sticking up. I'd have to let Donnalyn know so we could fix it together.

"When I got to my apartment, my family was looking at pictures of a house they liked," I said miserably.

"Oh." Lucas picked at another piece of linoleum and frowned.

"We can't afford to buy it. My mom said it was a daydream. But it made me realize we really are going to move eventually. I kept hoping that maybe if I could convince everyone how great it is here, they wouldn't want to leave. That we could stay here forever somehow. But we can't. And besides, staying here would mean my parents were stuck having money troubles forever. And I don't want that."

"Well, everyone leaves," Lucas said. "Why should you be any different?" He sounded more annoyed than blue. I knew the feeling. It was a mixture. And both feelings were rotten.

"I don't want to leave you two. Or Miss Beverly. Or Mrs. Johnson. Or Donnalyn. Or Mr. Stevens. Or anyone. I just don't!"

"No one wants to live here forever," Alice said.

"I do. Or at least, I did before I realized what staying here would mean for my family."

Alice and Lucas nodded. There was no way for all of us to be happy. It was either me or them. It didn't seem fair.

"If you had a choice to live somewhere else, would you?" I asked them.

Alice looked down at her lap and frowned.

"I'm sorry. I know you'd want to live with your mom."

"It's OK," Alice said. "Since we can tell each other anything, can . . . can I tell you both something? About my mom and why I've been so upset?"

We nodded.

"The reason she won't be coming back for a long time is because she got arrested." Alice closed her eyes and breathed in slowly. "She stole some money. For drugs, I guess. And now she's . . ." But Alice couldn't seem to go on.

I reached over and put my hand on her knee, trying to comfort her the way she had me. "She's what?"

"In this place that's kind of like prison," Alice said. "It's for people who commit crimes related to their drug problems. I didn't want to tell you because I felt ashamed. And then I felt ashamed for feeling ashamed." She breathed in again and opened her eyes.

It seemed no one really knew what to say. My chest ached for Alice. And for Mrs. Johnson, too. And Stevie.

"Grandma says, at least Stevie is off the streets and safe now. She has to go through a drug rehab program before she can be released. Maybe if she can recover, we can be together again. But it's going to take time.

That's what Grandma says. Everything takes so much time."

"I'm sorry," I said.

"Me too," Lucas added. "But I'm glad your mom is getting help. That seems . . . hopeful."

Alice nodded. "Let's change the subject now, though, OK? I don't want to think about it anymore."

"OK," Lucas said. "Well, to answer Ivy's question, if I could live anywhere, it would be someplace that made my dad happy. He used to dream of living in a little house on a lake. He says loons are his favorite bird and they make the most beautiful sound."

"I've heard them before!" I said. "They sing people to sleep at night sometimes. And wake them up in the morning."

"Really?"

"Yes. They go *oooh-oooh-ooh-oooh* in a pretty way."

I realized I'd never taken Lucas and Alice to the lake, like my mom had promised after our first fight at the pool. Maybe we could still go.

"Where would you want to live?" Lucas asked.

"Here, with you," I said. "Unless you moved to the lake. Then I'd want to live next door. And we could ride our bikes here to visit everyone and bring them treats."

"I wish it could happen."

I thought about how I'd been jealous of Lucas and Alice, because sometimes they were so close, they seemed like brother and sister. I'd wanted them to feel that way about me so badly. Now that seemed less important. What mattered was that they'd both welcomed me into their friendship. And now we were all best friends. And I loved them.

"Me too," I said.

We leaned against the kitchen cabinets and didn't talk for a while. In the other room, we could hear Mr. Stevens snoring peacefully.

"I'm sorry I hurt your dad's feelings when I suggested making him a chair," I said.

"It's OK. In some ways, I wish you could. I know you'd have made something really great. But it's not something he wants."

"I know. I hope he gets that scooter soon, though. Too bad I can't make one of those!"

"Ivy, you really are a good inventor," Alice said. "Maybe you *could* make one. Someday. Or maybe Donnalyn will find a broken one that you could fix! You can fix anything!"

"Yeah, Handy Girl!" Lucas said.

Alice leaned her head on my shoulder.

I wished it was true. But I knew now that there were some things that I couldn't fix.

Life's unfair, I thought. But I didn't say it out loud. It was just another saying. *Meant to be. Out of sight out of mind. Where there's a will there's a way. Blah, blah, blah.* I was tired of silly sayings.

"I wish things were different," I finally said. "Well, no. I mean I wish things could stay the same . . ." But then I thought of Alice, and that wasn't true, either. "No . . . I don't know what I want. Other than the three of us staying friends forever, no matter where we go."

It was the most true thing I could think of.

"Me too," Lucas said.

"Yes," Alice said. "That doesn't seem like such a hard thing, does it? To be friends forever?"

"I guess not," I said.

Lucas sat up straighter. "What do you mean, you guess not? Of course it's not. It's the easiest thing in the world!"

"Yeah!" Alice said.

They were right, of course. That was one thing that shouldn't be hard at all. And it was something that didn't have to change, no matter what happened! If anything was meant to be, it was being best friends with Alice and Lucas. Friends forever.

ꜟ Chapter Twenty-Eight ꜞ

Alice's bike was done. But to make it even more special, I needed Rachel and some top-secret planning to pull off the best surprise ever!

On the big day, I had everything packed, planned, and ready to go.

"This is a really long bike ride, Ivy. Are you sure?" Rachel asked me more than once.

"Yes! Yes! Yes!" I reassured her. "And you are the best sister in the world!"

"I already forgave you for not giving me the first bite of your cake like you promised," she said. "You don't need to keep buttering me up."

I smirked. "I'm sure I want Alice and Lucas to see the beach before summer's over. What better way than to ride bikes? It will be perfect."

"All right, then," Rachel said.

Inside, I still thought she was the best sister in the whole world, but I kept that thought to myself.

A whole week had gone by, and I'd had to secretly talk with Alice's grandmother to get permission for Alice to ride *and* secretly talk to Mr. Stevens to make sure Lucas was allowed to as well. I hadn't told Lucas about the bike because he wasn't the best at keeping secrets, especially when it came to treats! But I did have a long talk with Donnalyn and Mrs. Johnson to make sure they thought it would be OK to surprise Alice with the bike, even though she hadn't asked to be on the list. I explained why I thought she wanted to keep her old bike—because of Stevie. Mrs. Johnson said she could always keep her old one if it gave her comfort. But it would be nice to have one she could ride.

It wasn't easy sneaking around, but I'd found a way. It was a little embarrassing, but this surprise was worth it. When we were outside at the picnic table, I would tell Alice and Lucas I'd be right back because I had to go to the bathroom and instead would run up and do some fast-talking with Mrs. Johnson and Mr. Stevens to explain how careful we would be, and that Rachel would take us and it would be *perfectly fine*.

Seeing my family looking at future houses, I didn't know how much time I had left here. But I sure wasn't going to risk waiting for next summer!

I packed a picnic lunch for everyone and put it in my backpack, along with a thermos of lemonade. Since the new season of *Bake It to Make It!* hadn't started yet, the three of us had been meeting up to bake some of the recipes we'd found in *Larousse.* But today, I told them to meet me at Donnalyn's workshop for a big surprise.

One of the things that took the longest to find was a bike helmet for Alice. Donnalyn insisted I had to have a new one for her before I could give her the bike. I had called the people at the recycling center and asked them to be on the lookout, and they'd finally called and told me they had one, with the tags still on it and everything! I strapped the helmet to the handlebars and tied a ribbon on the bike. Now all I had to do was wait for Alice to arrive.

"You sure did a beautiful job on this bike," Donnalyn said. "I'm proud of you, Ivy."

"I hope Alice likes it!"

I could not stand still. I had the worst case of ants in my pants in my entire life!

I adjusted the ribbon for the ten thousandth time and stood back to see what the bike would look like from Alice's eyes when she came into the workshop.

"Would you stop fretting? You're making *me* nervous!" Donnalyn said.

She turned up the volume on her little radio and went back to a toaster oven she was trying to repair. She wiggled her hips to the music as she used a tiny screwdriver to take the oven apart. I started to do my own little dance around the bike, waving my hands in the air and jumping all around. But I still felt antsy!

"That's more like it!" Donnalyn said, laughing at my dance moves. She turned up the music, and I danced even faster.

"What's going on here?" a voice yelled above the music.

I jumped about a mile and turned to see Alice and Lucas standing in the doorway.

"You're here!" I hollered.

Donnalyn turned down the volume.

"Alice! Close your eyes right now!" I shouted, running over to them.

Alice closed her eyes. When Lucas saw the bike, his jaw dropped. I couldn't tell if it was a good shocked or an angry shocked.

Oh no.

Suddenly, I was scared. What if this plan backfired like some of my others? What if Alice got mad at me all over again? What if Lucas was mad I didn't fix up a bike for him, too?

Oh no. No, no, no!

I looked at Donnalyn, fear filling my chest.

Donnalyn gestured for me to go on.

I took a deep breath. I had to trust that I'd done the right thing. It was too late to turn back now!

I took Alice's hand and walked her closer to the bike. Lucas still looked shocked. I eyed the ribbon one more time.

Please let her love it. Please let her love it, I said to myself. I took one more deep breath and let it out slowly, like Rachel taught me. But my heart was beating so fast, I thought my whole body would start jumping around.

"OK, on the count of three, open your eyes, and you will get a big surprise! One . . . two . . . three . . . OPEN!"

I jumped aside, and Alice opened her eyes.

"Ta-da!" I sang.

Alice stood still, staring at the bike.

I couldn't tell what she was feeling. She kept standing there, not moving.

"It's for you," I said nervously. "I think the seat is adjusted properly, but you'll have to test it and see."

Lucas and Alice walked around the bike, inspecting every angle.

"It's OK if you don't want it," I said. "I know you like your old bike. You can keep that one, too. But this one will be easier for you to ride. And—"

"This is for me?" Alice interrupted. "I don't understand."

"I salvaged a bunch of parts from different bikes and put them all together to make one! Do . . . do you like it? It's OK if you don't."

Alice reached for the helmet.

"That's for you, too! Donnalyn said I couldn't give you a bike unless I had a proper-size helmet to go with it."

Alice put the helmet on and patted the bike seat, running her hand on it as if she was petting Rainbow.

I looked to Lucas, but he was no help. He still just stared and stared.

"Alice," I said. "Please. Say something!"

She finally looked at me, and a smile slowly filled up her whole face. "Holy smokes, Ivy!"

"Does that mean you like it?"

"We knew you were a handy girl, but we didn't know you were *this* handy!" Lucas said.

Alice walked around the bike again, touching the frame, the handlebars, the hand brakes.

"It's my favorite color," she said. "But . . . I do have a bike already. I know it's too small, but . . . my mom gave it to me when I was little. That's why I don't want to replace it."

"I understand," I said. "But you don't have to get rid of the old one."

"And this one you can actually ride!" Lucas said.

Alice looked unsure.

"Why don't you bring it outside and try it out?" Donnalyn said. "That thing's been taking up space in my workshop long enough. Get it out of here!"

I held the door open, and we wheeled the bike out of the workshop, down the hall, and out through the front doors.

"Stay on the sidewalk until you get the hang of that bike," Donnalyn said. "And, Ivy, make sure the seat is the right height."

Alice straddled the bike, then hesitated. She tilted her head at me.

"Don't forget to buckle your helmet," I said.

"This is the nicest present I ever got," Alice said. "I mean . . . the most thoughtful. It must have taken you ages."

"I like fixing things," I said. "Remember?"

"Yeah, Handy Girl, I do." Alice put her weight on the pedal and started moving forward. She wobbled at first, but then she was off like a shot. "Can't catch me!" she yelled as she glided away.

Lucas and I ran after her shouting, "Woo-hoo! Faster! Faster!" Then we hurried to the bike rack to get our own bikes and helmets and raced after Alice.

"Don't go too far!" Donnalyn shouted. "And yield to pedestrians!"

I waved at her and sped full steam ahead.

❧ Chapter Twenty-Nine ❧

After Alice got used to her bike, the three of us went inside to put our bathing suits on. I didn't tell them why, just to do it. When we met back outside, I asked them if they were ready for another big surprise, and of course, they were. Who wouldn't be?

"You need to stay close behind me," Rachel said after joining us with her bike. "If I pull way over on the shoulder, you do the same." She waited for us to nod in agreement. "All right, then, here we go!"

It was hot and muggy, and I was sweating within a few minutes. I kept looking back to make sure Lucas and Alice were right behind me.

"How much farther?" Alice asked when we stopped at a traffic light.

"We're almost there," Rachel said. "Are you all OK?"

Lucas gave her a thumbs-up.

"This better be worth it!" Alice said. She wiped her sweaty forehead with the hem of her shirt.

I felt a little nervous again. What if they didn't like the beach? What if they were disappointed?

"Oh, it's worth it," Rachel said.

She winked at me, and I immediately felt better.

"Have I ever steered you wrong?" I asked Alice.

She made a funny face, as if she was remembering the last time I asked her that and we made those ugly scallion doughnuts.

"Never mind. C'mon!"

When the parking lot came into sight, I let out a sigh of relief. "We're here! We did it!" I yelled.

We locked up our bikes and headed to Rachel's and my favorite spot at the far end. Micah was already there with his towel spread out. I ran over and hugged him. He seemed bigger than I remembered, and his hair was longer.

"You've changed!" I said.

"You too!" he said. "You're taller!"

"I am?" I stood on my tiptoes and measured the top of my head against his.

Micah laughed. "Cheater."

"Hi," Lucas said, coming up beside us.

"Do you remember Lucas and Alice?" I asked. "They're my best friends. You'd know that, but you hardly ever visit anymore."

"Don't be rude," Rachel said.

I smirked. "Let's swim!"

We all ran into the water except Lucas, who stood at the edge.

"What are you waiting for? The water's perfect!" I said.

"It is!" Alice made a splash with her foot.

Lucas took a small step forward.

"Lucas! You're not thinking about fish pee, are you?" Alice asked.

"More like poop."

"Oh, brother. It's *fine*," I said. "I've been swimming here my whole life, and a little fish poop never hurt me. Now, come in and play! It's fun!"

I went back for Lucas and took his hand, guiding him into the water.

When we were all up to our ribs, I gestured to the water below. "See how clean it is? Crystal clear."

"I guess so," Lucas said.

"I want to show you all the fun things we used

to do here. And I bet by next summer, we'll be old enough to ride our bikes here by ourselves! Won't that be great?"

"You probably won't even be here next summer," Lucas said. "Remember?"

"Lucas!" Alice scoffed. "Way to spoil the moment!"

I felt a nudge of anger, but then I realized, none of us really knew where we'd be a year from now. So why not live in the moment?

That was another funny phrase I'd heard. But in this moment, I kind of liked it.

I dove under the water and came back up with a mouthful and spit it in an arc at Lucas's chest.

"Hey!" Lucas said, shocked.

I giggled. "Can't catch me!" I dove back under and swam toward the rope line, pushing through the water. Rachel always said the most peaceful place was underwater at our beach, and I agreed.

The underwater sounds echoed in my ears. I opened my eyes and saw the rope line ahead. I pushed myself to swim faster. I was a little out of practice — it had been so long since I'd come swimming, but swimming was like riding a bike. Once you learn, you never forget. I found my rhythm and sped through the water. I was grinning from ear to ear as I reached for the rope. I felt happy from the top of my head to the tips of my toes. Maybe *this* would be the best day ever.

I turned and saw Lucas and Alice swimming toward me, and they were grinning like happy goofballs, too.

"I told you you'd love it here!" I called to them.

"Got it!" Alice said, tapping the rope with her fingers.

In the distance, the lifeguard's whistle blew. "Hands off the line!" she yelled.

"She always yells at us, but it's no big deal. C'mon! Let's go play Clueless with Micah and Rachel."

"What's Clueless?" Alice asked.

"It's a game we made up. You have to guess what the other person is saying underwater."

"Sounds weird," Lucas said.

"And fun!" Alice added.

We swam back toward shore and played with Micah and Rachel for a while, then we all collapsed on our towels on the beach and dried ourselves in the sun.

"I'm glad we came here, Ivy." Alice sat up and began playing in the sand, making a castle.

"Me too!" I hopped up and filled one of the cups I'd brought for lemonade with lake water, then poured some on the sand. I took a handful of wet sand and began to drip it onto the mound Alice had made.

Lucas joined us, and together we made an enormous drip castle at the edge of our towels.

"Not bad," Lucas said when we finished.

"Do you really think our cake looked anything like a drip castle?" I asked.

"I mean . . ." Alice started. She tilted her head one way, then the other. "I think our cake was nicer."

We all laughed.

"We'll have to keep coming back here to practice our real sandcastle skills," I said.

"But we'll still go to the pool, too, right?" Lucas asked.

"Of course. But there's less pee here," I said.

"Gross! Stop talking about pee!" Alice said.

"I'm glad we're all friends again," Lucas said.

"We've always been friends," Alice said. "I was just going through a hard time and needed some space."

"I wish we could have helped more," I said. "And I wish I'd known the right thing to say."

Alice shrugged and dug her toes into the sand. "Sometimes there aren't any words to make friends feel better. Sometimes you have to wait for them to come back to you. The important thing is to be there when they do."

I didn't say it out loud, but I thought again about

the phrase "meant to be" and how when you love someone, you have to let them go and hope they come back. I hoped someday Alice's mom would be able to come back. I hoped they were meant to be. Someday.

I closed my eyes and breathed in the smell and sound of the beach. Of this moment. I'd been waiting for this for a long time. And even though Alice would have to wait longer for her meant-to-be moment, I made a wish that it would come true.

"This is nice," Alice said.

Lucas dug his feet under the sand next to hers. "Yeah," he agreed.

I wiggled my toes. They had some green nail polish on them that was mostly chipped off. On the other side of me, Rachel and Micah were lying on their bellies, their backs warming in the sun.

This was better than nice, I thought. It was perfect.

I didn't know what changes were in store in the months ahead, or even tomorrow, but today it seemed we were all where we were meant to be: living in the moment and loving every minute.

Now, that was one saying I could get behind. And today, of all the sayings I knew, it seemed the most perfect, for this moment, right now.

Acknowledgments

This book would not have come to be without the patient and steadfast guidance of my editor, Joan Powers. When reading an early draft of *Where the Heart Is*, Joan left a sweet note in the margin of a scene about Ivy, noting, "Ivy needs her own book!" Thank you, Joan, for planting that seed—and for all the nurturing needed to help it grow. Thanks also to Barry Goldblatt for his early enthusiasm and constant support and friendship. As always, to my writing partners and dear friends, Debbi Michiko Florence and Cindy Faughnan, for their valuable feedback and love. If not for their daily check-ins and encouragement—through injury, pandemic, and the loss of loved ones—I fear I never would have finished. To my husband, Peter Carini, who reminded me why I write, how I write, and who I write for. Thank you to Pam Consolazio for another beautiful cover, which perfectly captures the heart of this story. And finally, to Jamie Tan, Anne Irza-Leggat, and the rest of Team Candlewick for the dedication and love you all put into making and promoting books for young people. I am forever moved by and deeply grateful for the work you do.